MURDERS AND GENEALOGY IN HENNEPIN COUNTY

A DETECTIVE ANNA FITZGERALD MYSTERY

PATRICK DAY

Pyramid Publishers
Buffalo, Minnesota

Pyramid Publishers
1314 Grandview Circle
Buffalo, MN 55313
763-390-4853
www.pyramidpublishers.com

Printed by
Lightning Source
1246 Heil Quaker Blvd.
La Vergne, TN USA 37086

ISBN – 978-0-9851514-0-9
LCCN – 2012932750

Cover and Interior Design and Layout by
Just Ink Digital Design

Printed in the United States of America

DEDICATION

I wish to dedicate this book to Marv Schaar, Uncle Marv in the story, whose depiction in *Murders and Genealogy in Hennepin County* is as close to the real Marv as I could possible make it. His genealogy of the Schaar family and who he thought was his great-aunt Gertrude served as the base genealogy of the story. From this base I wrote what would be classified as a story of historical fiction.

Marv Schaar suffers from muscular dystrophy and regales me every Saturday with his humor and joy of life. He lives in Park View Care Center, one of the best nursing homes I have ever set foot in.

ACKNOWLEDGMENTS

I sought for a real house in Hennepin County to serve as a model for the house Jakob Meyer built and to be the scene of his murder and the murder of Eldridge Gant some 141 years later. I thank Rebecca Mavencamp, the Director of the Rockford (Minnesota) Area Historical Society, for her offering of The Ames-Florida-Stork House for such a role, which was built in 1860 and portrays that era of time and the time of later additions. The rooms, furniture, and bookcases described in the book are all accurate depictions of The Ames-Florida-Stork House.

I would like to thank Detectives Sarah Phenow and Mary Jerde of the Hennepin County Sheriff's Office, Investigative Division, who were a valuable resource for me in my passion to be accurate with crime scene and investigative procedures, as well as the whole process of how the Sheriff's Office operates in Western Hennepin County and downtown Minneapolis. Sarah, Mary, and their supervisor, Lieutenant Todd Turpitt, were most kind in allowing me access to their facilities and answering about 100 questions.

Betty Dircks of the Heritage Center in Buffalo, Minnesota, is a genealogy guru who filled in the missing pieces of the story's genealogy thread and answered another 100 questions I had about the genealogy portrayed in the story. I came to feel that if Betty didn't know the answers to my questions, no one did.

After the narrative was reviewed chapter by chapter, Elizabeth Rajs of California edited the manuscript and rid it of clumsy sentences, tightened up various scenes, and made the book much more professional.

My friend, Jack Harrold, met with me at a coffee shop in Buffalo to go over every chapter I wrote and to make suggestions for the next chapter. He encouraged me to keep moving on when I might have put the project on a back shelf.

And there were others, too numerous to mention, who helped me with research, genealogy, and legal accuracy. I took the liberties afforded an author of historical fiction, but they were all within the framework of plausibility. My constant question to all my resources was, "Is this the way it would have happened?"

TABLE OF CONTENTS

CHAPTER ONE

THE MURDER OF ELDRIDGE GANT

I stood alongside Anna Fitzgerald when she took her first breath out of the womb. I will be standing by her when she takes her last breath on this earth. I am with her now in October 2006 as, at the age of thirty-four, she enters the home of Eldridge Gant.

Anna was on call that night when the phone rang at 8:02 p.m. She came from her flat in the Warehouse District of Minneapolis, driving her unmarked black Impala squad car, and was at the scene by 8:45 p.m. She wore her "power" outfit of blue slacks and a fashionable red sweater over a white blouse. On her belt was a .40 caliber Smith & Wesson M&P semi-automatic handgun, her badge, work cell phone, and a pair of handcuffs.

While she was driving to Rockford, the patrol deputy still at the scene called and updated her in detail about the crime, and gave her directions to the house. Anna would be the lead detective on this case, but she would need help. She paged out for additional detectives and soon had four others on her team, briefing them by radio about what she knew and asked Joe Wilshire if he would quickly get a search warrant from a judge on call. With her team identified and waiting for further assignments, she arrived at the home of Eldridge Gant.

Located on Bridge Street, on the Hennepin County side of the Crow River, the house was completed in the fall of 1860 by Jakob Meyer, added onto in 1890, and received a final addition in 1912. When the house was built in Rockford Townsite, it was on a farm with acreage to both the north and east. Now it stood in the middle of the city of Rockford, Minnesota, surrounded by homes.

Anna slowly drove on the gravel driveway to the back of the house, where the leaves of October lay fallen on the outside parking area, blown in swirls by a strong, cold wind that seemed to be announcing winter. She talked to herself. "This must be the right place with a sheriff's car back here."

The house was clad in 5 ½" hardwood siding with a 1" lap, painted white, and little more than a few boards had been replaced over the years. She entered the backdoor of the 1912 addition and walked through a summer kitchen into the regular kitchen.

The deputy had arranged a path of light to the crime scene to make it easy for her to follow. She passed through the dining room with its glowing chandelier, the music room with two lamps casting shadows on the piano, and into the brightly lit parlor of the original 1860 house.

Immediately to her left was a fireplace with a flooring of red bricks. The rest of the room was hardwood with a thin red rug partially covering it. In front of the fireplace, tied to a kitchen chair, sat the unfortunate Eldridge Gant.

Eldridge no longer inhabited this earth. Two hours earlier Mack Freighter and Toby Levias, men devoid of conscience, tied him to the chair, mercilessly tortured him, and set him on fire. Toby did most of the torturing and flicked his cigarette lighter at the lighter-fluid-soaked Eldridge. The two men quickly snuffed out the fire when he screamed he would tell them where the tin box was, but there is only so much a ninety-six-year-old man can take, and Eldridge had taken more of it than he could handle. He gasped out the hiding place through twisted lips set in a charred face. Then his head dropped to his chest where the fire was still smoldering through what was left of his shirt, and his body emptied itself into what was left of his pants.

Ed Simmers in the brown house to the east made the first 911 call. He was able to see the parlor fireplace and something on fire in front of it, though he didn't know the fuel source was Eldridge. The second call was from Mr. Kensington who lived in the cream-colored house to the north. He saw a light come on in the hallway window of the second floor and then in the two windows of the master bedroom and could see two men walking across the three windows, neither of whom was Eldridge. That made him suspicious.

The Hennepin County Dispatch in Golden Valley received the two 911 calls within minutes of each other. Hennepin County Sheriff's patrol car 1221 was already in Rockford and that deputy was at the crime scene in less than five minutes. He entered the back door, drew his revolver, and walked quietly up the stairs into the master bedroom. He surprised the two killers just as they were pulling out the wide, shallow tin box hidden underneath a floorboard in the southeast corner of the master bedroom, between the floorboard and the laths leading to the plaster ceiling in the room below. He quickly handcuffed them, and the tin box lay on the floor.

When the second deputy arrived from Medina ten minutes later, the first deputy threw the two handcuffed men into his squad car and headed out. The crime scene was sealed until a search warrant could be signed, allowing the crime lab, medical examiner, and Anna to start the investigation.

Mankind has made major advances in science, medicine, industry, and technology – but few advances in basic human decency. I witnessed a time when people could only walk from place to place, and years later a space ship reached the moon. Yet Mack and Toby were no different in character than Cain who murdered Abel. After many years, I have become cynical about the ongoing selfishness, greed, nastiness, and violence of the human race, which seems to have learned nothing from its past.

I saw it all. I always see it all. My name is Time. I'm not in the habit of writing and commenting on what I observe, but this is a compelling story that includes one of my favorite people – Anna Fitzgerald. You see, Anna has an understanding and appreciation of time that I appreciate. So many people live in their past, dwelling on mistakes and lost opportunities, and look ahead to their future with longing or dread. Anna has learned to live in the present moment and drink in the people she is with and the surroundings she is in.

Mankind in general has always seen me as the great enemy by the time they reach their twenties. Thousands of years of hard words spoken against me have hardened my heart. Yet there has always existed a remnant of good people, like Anna, who have cracked away at my hardness by their optimism, compassion, and love.

Anna has kept a journal since she was fifteen, and that's how I know so much about her, peeking over her shoulder at every page she writes. As St. Paul wrote in Philippians 4, verses 11 and 12, she has learned to be content in every circumstance and in every situation. There is much of me written in that journal.

I was there during an exchange Anna had with her mother the year before her father died, when her mother was unhappy that she was growing older. "I hate time, Anna. It's so cruel to thrust me into a season where each day my powers are diminished. I have nothing to look forward to but a nursing home."

Anna kindly looked her in the eyes and softly said, "Time's all you have, Mother, my dear; I love time, and I'll love time yet when *I* am sixty-eight. You see, Mother, time is life. You've been given time to live, and you need to make the best of every moment you're on this earth. I want you to be happy with all my heart. Look back to the positives in your life so far. Look at the family you have nurtured. Look forward not to what you can't do now but what you can still do. And know that I love you just the way you are."

Back at the crime scene, with the smell of burnt flesh still heavy in the air Anna looked at Eldridge with a mixture of horror and compassion, and spoke with sadness in her voice to the Hennepin County patrolman in the parlor. "I've never gotten used to this, Paul. I am so sick of scenes like this, and my blood is boiling with anger at the two men who tortured and murdered this old man. If I had arrived at the scene first and one of those cold-blooded killers had a gun in his hand, they'd both be on their way to the morgue right now, not jail."

The first deputy on the scene had already taken Mack and Toby back to the Grain Exchange Building in downtown Minneapolis, where the Hennepin County Investigative Division occupied the entire sixth floor. Anna called team member Sylvia Johnson and asked her to wait in the interrogation room until Mack and Toby arrived. "Sylvia, the two men you'll be interrogating don't deserve to live. Don't be kind to them in extracting information. I'm hoping we can wrap this case up quickly and send them off to prison for life."

The two men were ushered into the interrogation room on the sixth floor, between the room where all the detective cubicles were and the hallway that led to the conference room, case file storage, and Narcotics. The room was small, filled with electronic equipment and a hidden video system behind the north wall. Sylvia heeded Anna's words. She slammed the door shut after they were in the room, curtly apprised them they were being charged with first-degree murder, and formally Mirandized them. "You two hoodlums were caught red handed. It's not going to go well for you. I'd suggest you be as cooperative as you can. That'll be the only thing going for you. How did you know about Eldridge Gant and the hidden tin box?"

Sylvia had the gift to be really mean and threatening, and she exposed them to all her powers of intimidation. They just stared at her. Finally, Toby said, "We ain't talkin til we git a lawyer." That was the end of the questioning, and the suspects were hauled over to the new Hennepin County Jail right across the street. It was called The Public Safety Facility. Sylvia gave Anna a quick call and told her the two suspects had lawyered up and there was nothing else she could do. Anna responded to Sylvia, "There are a few things I'd like to do to those two before they meet with a lawyer, but then I'd be sharing a cell with them."

Anna disappoints me when she makes rash comments like that one or voices her desire to have shot Mack and Toby at the crime scene. Time would dispose of Mack and Toby appropriately, but Anna wanted at that moment to take matters into her own hands. She knew she couldn't, but just to say it…

The crime lab, medical examiner, patrol deputy, and Anna waited twenty minutes before receiving a call from Joe Wilshire. He had accomplished the unusual – a signed search warrant from a judge in just over an hour. The crime lab took pictures and a video of everything to record the original crime scene. While they were working in the master bedroom, Anna glanced down, and I could see the surprise on her face at the engraved name on the tin box – Jakob Meyer. After they were finished, she put on a pair of latex gloves, carefully opened the box, and let out a small gasp as she discovered about 150 gold and silver coins with Civil War dates, and a document from three banks dated May 30, 1864, stating the coins belonged to Jakob Meyer of Rockford Townsite.

A light escaped from her deep blue eyes, and I had a hunch what that light meant. A mystery had been revealed in her family when a third cousin of Anna's named Marv Schaar, the Schaar family genealogist, discovered a discrepancy in the birth date of Anna's great grandmother Gertrude Ackerman. With one date, Gertrude was the daughter of Anton Schaar of the Medina area by a second marriage. With another date, Gertrude was the daughter of Jakob Meyer of Rockford by a second marriage, the same Jakob Meyer whose name was on the tin box and the bank document.

My hunch was confirmed when I heard Anna say under her breath, "I think I'll make a visit to Uncle Marv. He might have information to shed light on this murder." As I mentioned earlier, Marv was really Anna's third cousin, sixty-six years old, with muscular dystrophy, and in a care center in Buffalo, Minnesota, ten miles from Rockford. Anna had met Marv at a family reunion five years previously and they became fast friends. Anna loved her cousin and affectionately referred to him as Uncle Marv. She visited him at least once a month.

Marv had ten books and several boxes of lineage and documentation of his family's genealogy. In his enthusiasm, he had shared just a small portion of it with Anna, but I saw the blank look on her face most of the time he was talking about genealogy. It's hard for someone who knows so much to communicate it to someone who doesn't have much interest in the subject.

If only I could speak to Anna, I could give her the information she needs to determine who belonged to whom and the disposition of all the characters, for I know the whole story. But I am just a reporter who can observe what happens, tell what is said, and make incisive comments to express my feelings and insights, and that's it. I hoped Anna could figure it all out, but there was no guarantee. There were so many pieces to work through, so many sources for finding information. Even Uncle Marv, with his genealogical expertise, could not figure it out. There are pieces missing to him that only I know about at this point.

But back to the murder. What were Mack and Toby doing in the house and what was the story behind the tin box? Since the two of them would not be talking to Anna or anyone else in the near future, I'll tell what I know of the matter.

Exactly ten years ago, Eldridge was in the sky parlor, so named by his father, a room to the left of the upstairs hallway. The sky parlor had three bookcases – one large one built into the southwest wall, a narrow one built into the northwest wall, and a horizontal one on the south floor. Eldridge was not one for much reading, but a book caught his attention – *Fifteen Decisive Battles of the World*, by Sir Edward Creasy. He started reading the book the way he always did. He paged through it with his thumb, flipping the pages one by one and skimming a bit of each page. That's how he determined whether he would read a book or not.

Between the fourth and fifth chapters, he encountered a surprise. There was a note from Jakob Meyer dated April 24, 1865, one month before he was murdered. The note said there was a tin box under the most southeast corner floorboard of the master bedroom. In the box were 150 gold and silver coins minted during the Civil War. He exchanged greenbacks that he had deposited in three St. Paul banks during the war for the gold and silver coins when he was mustered out of the service at Fort Snelling on April 29, 1864. Jakob didn't trust banks, so he eventually returned to St. Paul with the tin box in hand, received one statement signed separately by the three banks that such and such a value of gold and silver coins were his, and engraved the box when he got back to Rockford. He didn't want to be accused of stealing the coins, although that's exactly what he did, as we will see later.

Why did Jakob write a note in an obscure book as to where the money was? I heard Jakob talking to himself as he was writing the note. "This here's my retirement money and I ain't goin to tell Lizabeth bout it cause she may tell someun. I'll git a will drawn up for her that sez what book and page to look in for her inhertance, and I'll let a lawyer keep it." But Jakob never got to the will for reasons I will relate later.

Shortly after Eldridge discovered the note, his nephew Lucius was visiting as he did at least once a week. Eldridge trusted his nephew, showed him the book with the note in it, and even pointed out the floorboard referred to. He pledged Lucius to secrecy and revealed to him that he was named in a will as the heir of all Eldridge's assets.

Well, Eldridge was eighty-six years old and failing in intellectual capacity. His nephew Lucius was born without much intellectual capacity, so the two of them in their discussion of the matter talked about the $1,450 that Lucius would eventually receive, the face value of the coins in the tin box. Lucius didn't press Eldridge for more details. Neither of them figured out the coins were probably worth millions.

Lucius had a son, Jimmy, and one day in September 2006, ten years after his discussion with Eldridge, Lucius, in a state of alcoholic confusion, foolishly told Jimmy about the money hidden somewhere in Eldridge's house. Jimmy contacted a coin dealer and was informed the 150 coins were worth at least a million dollars, and he was determined to get that money from Eldridge. Jimmy immediately hired two thugs he knew from his drug-dealing business to go to Eldridge's house and force him to tell them where the tin box was, even if they had to rough him up a bit. Jimmy talked only to Toby and mainly by cell phone. That was not smart. He said he would give them five thousand dollars once the day was set for their visit to Eldridge and another five thousand when the tin box was safely in Jimmy's hands.

The morning after the murder of Eldridge Gant, Mack and Toby were questioned separately as to the name of their lawyer. Neither had an answer. The answer arrived ten minutes later – a lawyer named Jacob Gant, Jimmy's brother. He met with each of them separately and delivered a stark message. "You were caught in the act, your fingerprints and DNA are all over the instruments you used to torture Eldridge and on parts of his body that weren't burnt, so you are going to be found guilty. I'll do the best I can for you to receive the most lenient sentence, but that won't be easy. You won't be executed by the government, but you will be killed if you implicate anyone else in any way, right here in the jail if need be. We will fabricate a story that shows you in a better light than the heinous murderers you are. In the meantime, you don't talk to no one unless I approve it and I am there. And I mean no one. Do I make myself clear?" Both men had fear in their eyes and said they would follow his directions.

CHAPTER TWO

ANNA FITZGERALD
DETECTIVE

The morning after the murder, a Tuesday, October 17, to be exact, Anna parked her car underneath the Hennepin County Jail, ascended to ground level, and walked across the street to the Grain Exchange Building on the northeast corner of 4th Street and 4th Avenue. She passed through the swinging doors of the brownish stone building, walked briskly across the green marble floor to the elevators, as she observed the activity of the news stand on the ground floor.

Anna saw a woman walking slowly across the same green marble floor to the Grain Exchange offices and waved to her. "Mary, my dear, how are your treatments going? I pray every day you're going to beat this." Mary wistfully answered, "Oh, Anna, I wish that were true, but the doctors don't give me much hope."

"The doctors aren't in charge of you, Mary; God is. And I'm praying hard He'll heal you." Anna's encouragement and optimism put a smile on Mary's face. Some mornings, Anna's words were the only thing that kept her going. I know because that's what Mary told her husband.

Anna pushed the button for the 6th floor. One minute later, she stepped out of the elevator into a narrow hallway and turned right to Room 600M – Hennepin County Sheriff's Office Investigative Division. She opened the door, walked through the small waiting room, smiled at the receptionist and the handgun permit officer, and headed directly to the conference room for a 9 a.m. meeting with the members of her team. A fourth member had been added just that morning. Anna arrived fifteen minutes before the meeting and scribbled a list of action items to investigate the Eldridge Gant murder. "I may as well do something useful," she said out loud, though there was no one to listen. "I hate just killing time." Well, I sort of wish she hadn't said that, but I'm used to the colloquialism. It's sort of like people saying, "Damn you," without realizing what they are actually saying. If people really meant they wanted me killed, it would not go well for them. There are lots of foolish sayings in the English language.

Here's what Anna wrote:

1. Medical Examiner report
2. Crime Lab report
3. Obtain a search warrant for the cell phone records of Mack and Toby
4. Obtain a search warrant for the apartment that Mack and Toby shared
5. Check through their bagged clothes
6. Talk to residents in the apartment building who may know Mack and Toby
7. Talk to neighbors of Eldridge Gant, especially the two who called 911
8. Talk to people related to Eldridge, who is a bachelor
9. Find anyone else who might know Mack and Toby to determine if they had any connection to Eldridge
10. Determine the value of the 150 Civil War gold and silver coins

At this point Anna paused for a few moments, with an inquisitive look on her face, and lifted her head to speak to an empty room, "We need to determine who the Civil War coins belong to, and ethically I must let the team know there is a chance I may be a descendent of Jakob Meyer. I'll make that number 1.

"This'll be a useful crib sheet when we put the interrogation action items on the whiteboard," Anna pronounced. She often talked to herself out loud when no one was listening and sometimes when there were others nearby. Her co-workers were amused by her eccentricity.

The school-like wall clock buzzed at 9, and the team drifted in. The first was Joe Wilshire, who had obtained a search warrant for the Gant house so quickly; followed by Sylvia Johnson, who had questioned Mack and Toby until they lawyered up; and then Tony Talridge, who was a seasoned detective with twenty years of experience in the division. Finally, at exactly 9:05, Michael O'Hara dragged in, five minutes late as usual. Anna said with a mix of frustration and humor, "Michael O'Hara! Just because you're Irish doesn't mean you can saunter in any time you feel like it."

Mike responded with the Irish brogue he assimilated in County Kerry before coming to America with his family at the age of fifteen, "Oh, Anna, my sweetheart, what's the purpose of being Irish if there aren't a few special privileges allowed for the race. If you were 100 percent Irish instead of three-quarters, you could claim the same allowances." Anna couldn't help but laugh.

Anna's father was William Fitzgerald, who was taken two years before by lung cancer. Her mother was Maggie McGrath, who succumbed a year later of the same disease. She no longer needed to worry about becoming old and living in a nursing home. The couple was married in 1964 in St. Paul, and Anna was born February 4, 1972. Her maternal grandparents were both still alive, but those on her father's side were both dead. With names like Fitzgerald and McGrath, you might assume Anna was 100 percent Irish. But her paternal great-grandmother and great-grandfather were both 100 percent German. Their daughter, Anna, for whom our Anna was named, married Michael Fitzgerald in 1926, the parents of William who married Maggie. Through that lineage, Anna emerged as 75 percent Irish and 25 percent German.

Over the next two hours, Anna briefed her team on the pertinent details she knew about the murder of Eldridge Gant, including her possible connection to Jakob Meyer via information from Uncle Marv, and they all completed an extensive list of investigative items on a whiteboard. They were about to proceed through a rather formal assignment process, when Michael O'Hara held up his hand. "Anna, my darling, the ownership of the Civil War coins will be a major effort that you have an inside track on. I'd suggest you tackle this part of the investigation yourself."

Anna was quick to respond, "But Michael, wouldn't that be a conflict of interest for me?"

Tony Talridge answered the question while Michael was thinking. "Anna, I've seen something like this before. You have been open with information from your Uncle Marv. But there is no certainty you are an heir. Why don't you keep us apprised with where this piece of the investigation is heading and where you fit in? Then we can decide whether there is a conflict of interest."

Sylvia Johnson piggy-backed on what Tony had said. "Given that the information right now resides with your uncle and his genealogical searching, and given that you already know somewhat the possibilities of ownership, it doesn't make sense for any of the rest of us to be assigned to this. We trust you to do what is right."

Joe Wilshire was the last to speak, which was usually the case, not because he was shy but because he analyzed the information presented and was uncanny in framing the issue. I had seen him perform that role many times in investigations. When he spoke, people listened. "Anna, let me define what conflict of interest would mean for you. If you discovered that all or part of the money in the tin box were yours, and if you were planning on keeping that money, and if your investigation became thus in your own best interests, then you are smack into conflict of interest and would need to take yourself off that part of the investigation. I'd suggest that be your guide."

The rest of the team applauded Joe, and there were several "bravo" comments made.

"I really appreciate the way you are able to come up with a simple clarification of a complex issue, Joe." At that point, Anna walked around the table and put her hand on Joe's shoulder. "Will you write that down for me, Joe, so it can be my guide, and I promise all of you that I will abide by that definition?"

The five detectives assigned themselves to at least five items apiece, doubling or tripling up on those pieces that would take the most time. Though they would be in contact with one another during the week, the next scheduled meeting was for Friday morning. The investigation had begun.

I appreciated the methodical way the team launched the investigation. A written plan makes the best use of time. Too many of the human species act as if they have an attention deficit disorder –

jumping from one thing to another like drunken kangaroos, and it saddens me to see them so murderously massacring time.

I watched Anna write in her journal later that evening, "I expect Mack and Toby weren't the only ones involved in this crime, but I didn't want to prejudice the team by revealing my suspicions. It's best they start with a clean slate. Those two will be prosecuted simply and surely, but I want the mastermind behind this murder. I won't rest until the last 'i' is dotted and the last 't' crossed. We owe that to Eldridge. We owe that to the citizens of this state. Daddy, I wish you were here to call on. The two of us would be able to figure it out."

Before going to bed, Anna called Gramma and Grampa McGrath, as she did at least once a week. They were both in their mid-eighties. There was small talk about Gramma being over her cold and Grampa dealing with a case of identity theft. She was his coach in that awful circumstance.

Then Anna asked, "What do you know about Jakob Meyer?" Grampa, who was the McGrath family genealogist, spoke first. "After Marv told us about the different dates for the birth of your great-grandmother, Gertrude Ackerman, I spent some time at the Minnesota Historical Society Library just for curiosity. It seems to me you are as likely to be descended from Jakob Meyer as from Anton Schaar. I don't know anything more about Jakob Meyer than that. You'll have to ask Marv for more details." He started to ask why Anna wanted to know about Jakob, but his wife cut him off.

"How are you doing, Anna, my angel?" queried Gramma McGrath. "Have you seen that nice Jack Quinn lately?"

"I'm doing fine, Gramma, and I talk to him on the phone now and then, but we haven't had a date for over a year. I think I still love him, but my job keeps getting in the way. Right now I'm working on a gruesome murder that took place in Rockford. It seems like a simple case, but my instinct tells me it will be a major time consumer."

Her grandmother said sadly, with an obvious deep love for her granddaughter, "Anna, when you are lying on your death bed, you'll not be saying, 'Oh, I wish I had spent more time at my job.' You'll be saying, 'I wish I had married Jack and raised a family.' It's relationships that count, my sweet, not jobs. Make your life count for those you love now and the children you will love. You don't have to give up your job. You simply have to place it in the right spot – second."

There was silence for about ten seconds before Anna responded. "Gramma, I know in my heart you are right. That deathbed scene hit me like a slap in the face. I need to do some serious thinking and make changes. Thanks for your advice and for your love for me."

Anna went to bed resolved to rearrange her job and her love life.

Earlier I mentioned the depravity of the human race made me cynical. But there are bright spots here and there, such as Anna Fitzgerald. She is an overall good person, with only a few faults that disappoint me. But no one on this earth has ever been perfect, except One.

I notice, for the most part, that beautiful women have distinctive character flaws, two being pride and vanity. Although Anna is strikingly beautiful, with her oval face and high cheekbones, she is yet a modest person about her looks, but very confident in her ability to get things done.

When she was fifteen years old and her beauty evident, I watched her write in her journal, "I feel embarrassed when people say I'm pretty or beautiful. I don't think of myself that way. I'd rather have people say I'm kind or good or fair or honest. Those are the characteristics I admire, not beauty. Those are the words that describe my father."

Anna is five-foot seven-inches tall with a slender, muscular build, a throwback to her tomboy growing-up years. Her eyes are dominant, steely blue, and piercing. Criminals feel she is looking right through them. She also possesses one particular trait you would not expect. There is something in her bearing that tells criminals and co-workers that you don't want to mess with her.

Two years ago, Anna described herself in her journal. "I love my job as a detective, but I hope I never become hardened to crime and lose my compassion for people. I love God for creating me, I love my parents, I love life, I love those I work with, and I love the people I come in contact with (it's hard to love the hardened criminals, though I know that's what God expects of me). I should say this is how I'd *like* to describe myself, but I fall short of the mark too often to say unequivocally, 'This is who I am.'"

Anna's father was a prosecuting attorney for the city of Minneapolis for twenty-eight years, until he died at the age of sixty-two. His forte was prosecuting murderers. When Anna was about ten, she slowly became interested in her father's occupation; and he discovered it helped him frame a case when he explained it to her. His wife was not particularly interested in her husband's career, so it became a bond between Anna and her father to "figure out" crime scenes and murder cases.

For two years, Anna listened to her father and asked a basketful of questions. By the time she was twelve, their conversations had become more two way. Anna continued to ask questions, but she also initiated suggestions as to motives and methods, and figured out crime scenes as well as a seasoned investigator. Her father had gained another voice that made him a better prosecutor. It was a mark of his humility that he was willing to accept advice from a young girl. He praised her for being so precocious and called her his "little detective."

When "America's Most Wanted" started on TV in 1988, Anna, who was sixteen at the time, became an avid viewer, and her interest in criminal investigation blossomed. However, she wrote in her journal when she was eighteen that, "I'd like to be the detective Daddy says I could be, but my friends tell me that's not a career for a woman." Her tomboy ways had disappeared by the time she was a sophomore in high school, when she became interested in boys and being more feminine. Yet...her journal revealed there was a conflict within her whether to follow her destiny or listen to what others expected.

She hedged her bets when she attended college at the University of Minnesota. She selected a double major that could lead to police work but also held other options for employment. In 1994, she graduated with a B.A. in Sociology and a B.A. in Health and Physical Education.

By 1996, after two years working in her father's law office as a paralegal doing investigative work, she wrote in her journal, "My friends advise me to be a doctor, my mind summons me to be a lawyer like Daddy, but my heart calls me to be a detective. I'm going to listen to my heart."

She spent sixteen weeks at The Center for Criminal Justice and Law Enforcement Professional Licensing Program in Energy Park in St. Paul, completing the skills courses she needed and a few classroom courses. The program takes two years for someone without a college degree. She not only had the degree, but her college curricula met many course requirements of the program.

Once finished with her courses and skills training, Anna was licensed as a deputy sheriff for the Hennepin County Sheriff's Office Investigative Division. She commenced her career as a detention deputy in the Hennepin County Jail, one of two options available to those starting out; the other option was courts. She wrote, "I would have preferred courts, but face-to-face contact with criminals will probably be a better track for my ultimate goal – becoming a detective."

Anna worked two years as a detention deputy, and then transferred to Narcotics for four years. I could tell she enjoyed the undercover work, probably because it resurrected her tomboy instincts. She was the only female in that division, and she worked mainly with male drug pushers. I stood alongside her, as I often did, when she was writing in her journal. "If my ultimate passion wasn't to be a detective, I could see spending a few more years in Narcotics. But I have my five years of experience in now, six to be exact, and it's time to take the final jump."

The day after writing that entry, Anna threw open the door of the Hennepin County personnel department and filled out the forms to take her detective's exam, which consisted of a series of tests and more than one interview. This was a rigorous exam, and someone who was not competent or confident would not pass. Anna was thoroughly successful at every step and within two weeks she heard that she had accomplished her dream. As I stand with her right now, she has been a detective for four years. Her business card reads Anna Fitzgerald on the top line and Detective on the second line.

You might say she is married to her job...and not otherwise married. Many suitors have aspired to a romantically connect with her, but they all faded quickly when they realized they were second to her job – the odd hours, being called to a crime scene from a candlelit dinner, and regularly putting in sixty-hour weeks. It didn't seem to me that being a loner on the social scene was particularly troublesome, but on her thirty-fourth birthday she wrote in her journal, "Alas, the chances of marriage for me are becoming slim. Irish women are not meant to be old maids."

The boyfriend who stuck with her the longest was Jack Quinn, a lawyer with a large law firm in St. Paul, and an avid genealogist. I know from reading her journal over her shoulder that if there were anyone she would marry, it would be Jack. I wonder what she would think if she knew there was someone watching every word?

Anna first met Jack one week after she was promoted to detective. He was representing a fourteen-year-old young man who had robbed a grocery store in Medina. Anna was called as a prosecuting witness because she had investigated the case. Jack lost that one, and Anna approached him in the courtroom and jokingly asked if he wanted to help her celebrate the Hennepin County victory over supper. Jack laughed. "I'll take you up on that but only on one condition – I'll pay."

Anna was trapped. Jack took her to Murray's, seven blocks away on 6th Street. It was a steakhouse of high reputation and more extravagant than anything Anna was used to. They seemed to know Jack and gave him the most secluded table they had, at the very back of the restaurant, in front of the piano (which was played only on Friday and Saturday evenings). That was their first date. I know "love at first sight" is a trite phrase, but that's what it was. Anna was a beautiful woman and Jack a handsome man – tall, with a squarish face and strong chin, and a personality that was almost a perfect complement to Anna's.

Many romantic meetings followed over the next year. I must indulge in another trite observation, but it is true – they were sweethearts. You see, Anna and Jack were both good Catholics, and so lovers was not the applicable term for them, but it was close. Jack proposed marriage six months after they met; he said she was his true love and he wanted to live with her for the rest of his life. Anna was not ready for marriage; she said she wanted to settle down in her career first.

By the end of their first year of dating, Anna increasingly became swallowed up by her work, the meetings with Jack became more and more rare, and Jack was becoming more and more frustrated. On the anniversary of their first date, Jack took Anna home after supper at Murray's and went up to her flat with her as was their custom. When the door was closed, Jack lit into Anna before she even had a chance to take her jacket off. He was too kind to berate her in the restaurant.

"Anna, I'll not be playing second fiddle to your job one more day. Either we have a relationship or we don't. Either you decide to marry me or you don't. I'm not going to sit around waiting for you any longer to make up your mind."

Anna was too stunned to respond. Jack picked up a magazine from an end table and hurled it across the living room into the kitchen. It landed neatly on the top of the refrigerator. Then he turned around, opened the door, and slammed it shut with such force that the walls rattled and pictures fell over. Anna stood there with her coat on and cried.

For two months she didn't hear from Jack. Then he called for a date and she gladly accepted. But things were not the same. There was a coldness between them that resulted from the nasty scene that had occurred in Anna's flat. Every couple of months, Jack would call Anna, hoping that perhaps things were different with her job, but they were not. Sometimes they talked on the phone for an hour; sometimes they went out for dinner. They definitely no longer acted like sweethearts.

At the conclusion of their second year, they went once more to Murray's. As Jack was paying the check, he slowly spoke an apparently rehearsed proclamation, "Anna, it's too hard on me to see you or talk to you so infrequently. I had hoped your passion for your job would change to let me into your life. I'd suggest we stop seeing each other until your job is transformed into second place to our relationship." Once again, Anna couldn't respond. She was stone-faced until Jack let her off at her flat. Then she stood outside and cried.

After Jack, Anna's pattern was a few dates followed by another lost boyfriend. Jack dated various women for various lengths of time, but Anna was his benchmark, and everyone else fell short.

Anna missed Jack and called him now and again; he never called her. They would engage in small talk about what was happening in each other's lives, but they never met for supper or anything else. Anna was hoping Jack would suggest they get together and she'd show him their relationship was more important than her job. But that didn't happen.

"Hope springs eternal in the human breast," Alexander Pope said in a poem. Anna wrote in her journal of her hope that she and Jack would become friends again and then lovers. She was ready to marry him. Jack walked around his apartment periodically muttering, "Oh, Anna, my love, my love. How I long for you." But neither of them spoke those words to each other.

Anna rarely had a murder on her plate in her four years as a Hennepin County detective, which seems strange granted that in 1995 the New York Times changed the name of Minneapolis, Hennepin County, Minnesota, to "Murderapolis" after ninety-nine homicides. The year 2006 was predicted to reach sixty homicides at the most, and the word "Murderapolis" had long been discarded.

But Minneapolis, like most big cities, has its own detective and homicide divisions within its Police Department; as do the larger suburbs. That leaves the outlying areas of Hennepin County –towns, townships, and small cities – to contract with Hennepin County for patrol and detective services, such as Rockford and Medina (where the second officer on the scene of Eldridge Gant's murder patrolled). Regardless, her experience in her father's law office and her tough years in narcotics put her in first place within the department for investigating murders. The more usual caseloads were thefts, armed robberies, embezzlements, sexual assaults, domestic assaults, and a few DOAs that needed sorting out (but were not murders). In short, Anna's division handled anything a patrol deputy encountered that was not a traffic case.

That's my picture of Anna Fitzgerald as I know her, but it's time to return to the murder of Eldridge Gant and the tin box full of gold and silver coins.

CHAPTER THREE

JAKOB MEYER AND THE CIVIL WAR COINS

If Anna Fitzgerald is one of the verdant gardens in my assessment of mankind, Jakob Meyer is a blight on the landscape of history.

On October 19, 1850, I was there in Boston when Jakob Meyer of Biddeford, Maine, twenty-three at the time, married sixteen-year-old Rebecca Jane Griffin. Rebecca had been raised in Portland, Maine, and that's where she first became acquainted with Jakob. He was laboring there as a carpenter and living in her mother's boarding house.

Rebecca had moved to Boston when she was fourteen to work in her uncle's department store. She had an unfortunate affair with one Charles Gravely, which abruptly came to an end in the summer of 1850, when Jakob arrived in Boston and looked her up. Charles Gravely was looking to end the affair with Rebecca anyway, and Jakob's arrival in Boston was his path of escape. Jakob had fled Portland before the police could calculate he was the man in an alley outside Rey's Bar who killed a bar patron in a fight – by smashing him in the back of the head with a hammer before his opponent turned to face him. Jakob landed a good job in Boston building houses, and he was ready to settle down and get married.

Within two months after their marriage, Jakob compelled Rebecca to tell him about the affair with Gravely, for reasons that will come to light later. He called her a whore and treated her with such contempt that within three years she had a complete psychotic breakdown (what was simply called insane at the time). Jakob committed her to an insane asylum back in Augusta, Maine, in 1854, where she resided until her death in 1880. Rebecca had a deep hatred of Jakob for what he did to her and changed her name in the asylum to Jennie Gravely. She was never quite the same, though she became a model patient and lived a quiet life, not bothering anyone, not talking to anyone.

A daughter, Eva Meyer, was born into their marriage in 1851. When Jakob hauled her mother off to the insane asylum, he took Eva to Rebecca's uncle in Boston because he wanted no part of raising her. Eva lived with that family until 1865, when she left for Augusta to be close to her mother. Her mother passed her passionate hatred for Jakob onto her daughter, but it was not a hard sell. Eva was already ill disposed to him. She kept his last name, but adopted Jennie for her middle name – Eva Jennie Meyer.

What does all this have to do with the murder of Eldridge Gant and the lineage of Anna Fitzgerald? Those who pay attention to the five paragraphs above will be handsomely repaid as these two mysteries unfold.

I have observed with both humor and disdain that history often repeats itself. On a dark night at a German bar in downtown Boston in 1858, Jakob and a mean-looking drunk named Karl engaged in a violent argument about nothing significant. Jakob also was in an inebriated state and suggested they go out back and settle their differences like men. As in the Portland altercation, his opponent led the way out to the proposed battleground. But before Karl turned around with fists raised, Jakob yanked a hammer out of his work clothes, and bashed his head in with such force that the hammer became embedded in Karl's skull. Jakob ran away from the scene of the crime without his trusty hammer.

In the Portland bar fight, no one was aware Jakob and another man had gone outside to fight. In Boston there were fifty people who heard the shouting argument and saw the two men leave by the back door to settle their difference like men. Some even went outside to watch the fight, but the only action they saw was Jakob running down a back alley. They beheld the fallen Karl and deduced Jakob was the murderer, but no one knew who he was or his name; it was his first visit to that bar.

This was one of those times when I wished I could manifest myself to the onlookers and tell them who Jakob was and where he lived. As I revealed to you before, I can't see into the future, but there was no doubt in my mind that night that Jakob had more mischief to inflict on humankind, and history proved I was right.

The next morning Jakob packed up and headed west, all the way to Minnesota. Why Minnesota, so far away? Well, six months before the murder in Boston, Jakob was in a poker game at an acquaintance's house; and to cover a bet, the owner of the house arose from the card table, went into his bedroom, and came back with a bounty land certificate he had received from fighting in the Mexican War. The certificate was for 160 acres in what had become Rockford Township, just east of Rockford Townsite in the county of Hennepin. Jakob won the pot, and the man signed over the bounty land to him. It was a meaningless piece of paper then, but most fortuitous for Jakob when he needed a place of escape far away.

Jakob brought that certificate to the Bureau of Land Management in St. Paul, Minnesota, and was registered as the new owner of the quarter section of land.

Jakob built a small shack for himself while he constructed the house that later became the scene of the murder of Eldridge Gant. Then he transformed himself from a carpenter to a farmer.

On January 16, 1861, Jakob married Elizabeth Kohler of Franklin Township in Wright County. The marriage certificate was handwritten, since state or county official records were not in existence in 1861. The top of the page said, "Marriage Certificate." It was signed at the bottom by Rev. Henry Singenstree. He wrote,

> I the undersigned a minister of the Gospel did join in the holy bonds of matrimony according to the laws of this state Mr. Jakob Meyer of Hennepin County and Miss Elizabeth Kohler of Wright County after having examined both parties and becoming satisfied that there was no legal impediments thereto.

"No legal impediments thereto?" What did Jakob say to the minister about his first wife, if anything? Did Jakob even tell Elizabeth he had been married previously and had a daughter by that marriage? Well, I was there, so I know the answer to those two questions, but I'll leave it to Anna-the-Detective to discover the truth. After all, this is her story.

That spring, Jakob was too poor to start farming, so on April 25, 1861, after only three months of marriage, he enlisted in the First Minnesota Volunteer Infantry Regiment for three years or the duration of the war, whichever came first. Jakob signed up for the $100 federal bonus and $13 a month in pay. He, like most people in both the North and the South, thought the war would be over in short order. Jakob reckoned by the time he finished training at Fort Snelling in St. Paul, he would be sent home with his war money and still be able to put in a crop. How dreadfully wrong he was. The First Minnesota was involved in 61 engagements, including 34 battles, and numerous skirmishes that slaughtered the majority of the thousand men who were mustered in on April 29, 1861, and left only a small number to be mustered out on April 29, 1864.

Elizabeth was left to fend for herself back at the farm. Jakob did not share any of his war money with her. While most of his comrades sent money back home, she was forced to return home to Franklin Township until Jakob came back from the war. Her love for Jakob was compromised.

The initial battle for the First Minnesota was Bull Run on July 21, 1861. Jakob escaped alive, though first blood had been shed in his regiment. Jakob was greatly affected by the terror of men being struck down by .58 caliber bullets that were soft lead, about one inch in length. Even if one of those bullets entered a man's arm or leg, bleeding to death was ever at hand if a medical team did not intervene within minutes.

Jakob sent a letter back to Elizabeth that showed the degree of his fright, "Lizabeth, I'm scared of dieing on a battlefield far from home. I'm goin to do whatever I have not to git killed. I mis you and hope to git home soon."

I'll cover just two of the battles of the "War of Rebellion" as it was called in the North and "The War of Northern Aggression" as it was called in the South, to expose the pathetic means by which Jakob avoided death – Antietam and Gettysburg.

The First Minnesota was camped on Pry's Farm on the morning of September 17, 1862, located on Antietam Creek in the far northeastern corner of the battlefield. The battle began early in the morning and raged on until 9 o'clock in the evening. I watched the carnage with tears in my eyes. The fields of battle were a scene of death and suffering of an intensity I had rarely witnessed. The lines of battle brought men within 50 yards of one another as they blazed away as fast as they could reload.

Artillery loaded with double loads of canister ripped men to pieces. Shell fragments tore through the bodies of men like the effect of the first trumpet of Revelation – when hail and fire mixed with blood was hurled down upon the earth. Rifle barrels became so hot they were rendered useless. Screaming and whistling projectiles burst through the air as the peaceful scene of early morning turned into one of destruction, agony, and gore.

The First Minnesota waded across Antietam Creek and into the jaws of death. Passing through the East Woods they were greeted by the sight of dead and wounded under every tree. This is where Jakob drew the line. He was in the back row of the First Minnesota. The battle was so fierce in front of them that no one noticed when Jakob just lay down with the dead and pretended to be one of them. The First Minnesota was pummeled by 12 pound Napoleon cannons and a volley of musket fire that descended on their ranks like a blanket of lead. Before they were totally annihilated, they were reinforced by Union troops with artillery that drove the Confederate forces off the field of battle like frightened wild animals being hunted down by a pride of lions. As the First Minnesota marched back to their camp the way they had come, in the dark of night, Jakob slipped into the ranks and no one realized he did not fight alongside of them all day.

Gettysburg was fought July 1-3, 1863, and was the most critical battle of the war. On July 2, the First Minnesota was ordered into position in the line of battle near the center of the Union lines. About 7 p.m., some 300 men of the First Minnesota were ordered to charge and stop the advance of approximately 1,600 Alabama troops threatening to break through the line.

When Jakob saw his unit was outnumbered by more than five to one, he drew the line again. As they passed a field where dead bodies lay, Jakob hid among them and let his comrades face the rebel troops. In less than five minutes, 70% of Jakob's unit was on the ground, dead or wounded. It was like the Charge of the Light Brigade, which pales in comparison to the First Minnesota's charge "into the jaws of death, into the mouth of hell."

Reinforcements arrived after five minutes and the day was saved. The First Minnesota was ordered to retreat to the rear, and on the way back, in the dusk, Jakob once again slipped back into his regiment without anyone realizing he had not been with them in the charge. The confusion had been too great to keep track of who was there and who was not.

As if pretending to be dead was not cowardly enough, Jakob ransacked the bodies and stole the money they had on them – more than $5,000 during those two battles. Paymasters for Union troops paid their troops in paper money every three or four months. Jakob was lucky. Antietam and Gettysburg both occurred shortly after the troops had been paid for four months – $52 for privates, $676 for captains, up to $3,320 for a three-star general. Had his fellow troops realized what he was doing, they would have hung him from the nearest tree. Jakob obviously could not have carried that much money on him, so he sent it to three different banks in St. Paul, so as not to raise suspicion.

When the First Minnesota was mustered out on April 29, 1864, Jakob went to the three banks and exchanged the majority of the paper money, at a nearly 3:1 exchange rate, for $1,450 of newly minted gold and silver coins. I heard him tell one of the bankers, "I reckon I better make the exchange now. Greenbacks will go the way of Confederate paper money after the war, and these here gold coins will go no place but up. This here'll be my pension when I retire from farmen." He kept the 150 coins in the three banks for a few months before returning with a tin box to collect them, which is the one that was found in Eldridge Gant's home the night he was murdered.

One year and one month from Jakob's mustering out of the service and the ill-gotten gains of his battlefield cowardice, he died a mysterious death on May 24, 1865. This was a case where a bad man came to a bad end. It doesn't always happen that way, but I always have a sense of satisfaction when it does. I have a passion for justice.

Anna had chosen the assignment of valuing the 150 gold and silver Civil War coins. She signed for the tin box from the evidence room and transported it to a rare coin dealership in Minneapolis, where she had made an appointment with the dealer for 2 p.m. and had explained to him the nature of the visit. Michael O'Hara made the trip with her, armed with a shotgun and an automatic rifle. "Anna, my love, you are marvelously protected with me riding shotgun." Anna responded with a howl of laughter, "Michael, you impetuous Irishman, I'm more afraid of your shooting me by accident, or yourself, than any thieves who may try to strip us of this tin box." Michael smiled and shrugged his shoulders.

Anna identified herself and Michael as Hennepin County detectives, and opened the tin box. The coin dealer's polite demeanor turned into unbridled excitement when he saw the coins. "These are in mint condition," he said. "I've never seen this many coins in this excellent of condition. Where'd they come from?"

"I can't give you that information," said Anna. "This is from a criminal case that's still open."

From excitement, the coin dealer's features turned to anxiety as he took in the shotgun and rifle that Michael had carried into the store. Michael saw his concern and tried to make light of it. "Just pretend I'm not here, but if anyone comes into this store looking for trouble, we'll need a wheelbarrow to haul out his pieces."

The dealer did not think Michael's remarks were very funny. "It will take me a couple of hours to determine the value of the coins."

"We'll be right by your side," smiled Anna. "This is evidence we can't let out of our sight."

And so the three of them withdrew to the back room, took the coins out of the tin box, and matched them up against a list the dealer possessed of the value of Civil War gold and silver coins. It was simpler and less time consuming than the dealer had stated because many of the coins were similar and all coins were minted in the years 1862 and 1863. There were sixty $20 gold coins worth $1,019,250; forty $5 gold coins worth $808,000; and fifty silver dollars worth $645,000. The grand total was $2,472,250.

The face value of the 150 coins in 1864 was $1,450. Because many similar coins were lost or taken out of circulation by the Federal government, and the passing of 140 years, the market value of the coins increased seventeen-hundred fold. Anna received a signed appraisal from the dealer and took the coins back to the heavily-locked evidence room on the sixth floor of the Grain Exchange Building where the evidence officer of the division put them into a safe.

That evening, I watched Anna writing in her journal, "What a hell of a day! In my wildest dreams, I would never have guessed those coins were worth that much. There is now a high-stakes genealogy mystery tied into the murder of Eldridge Gant. Who is the rightful heir to those coins, and where did a poor farmer accumulate that much money? I'll drop in on Uncle Marv tomorrow, and this time I'll listen as he explains the genealogy of Gertrude Ackerman, my great-grandmother. What's the likelihood that her father was Jakob Meyer and what does that mean for whom the coins belong to? And if Gertrude's father is Anton Schaar, how does that play out? This case won't be over until the rightful heir to the 2 ½ million dollars is determined."

Well, I know what Uncle Marv knows, and Anna will be surprised by what the possibilities are. By what she wrote, I reckon she is naïve about how she might fit into all this.Unfortunately, Marv has never been able to find all the information he needed to close the case. He knows only possibilities and rumors, and now living in a care center, he is no longer able to do the active genealogical work needed to unravel the mystery.

CHAPTER FOUR

ANNA VISITS UNCLE MARV

It was Thursday, October 19, when Anna shut off her car in the parking lot of Park View Care Center in Buffalo, one hour from her office in downtown Minneapolis. Traffic had been light.

The automatic doors at the front entrance opened suddenly, and Anna walked into a glass entryway; then walked through another door leading into the hub of the facility. Marv Schaar's room was not far away, at the end of Main Street that starts at the hallway to the west and ends halfway down the hallway to the south. Marv, whose room was in the southern section, was steadily moving down the debilitating path of muscular dystrophy.

Anna was well acquainted not only with the facility but also with many of the staff. She said hello to the two nurses in the station right in front of her and stopped to talk to Emily – an attractive black nurse that was the most positive person in Park View.

"Emily, how are you so upbeat every day with the sadness of this place: people dying left and right every week and those like Uncle Marv?"

"Because I see every resident here as a glass half full, not half empty. I don't view your Uncle Marv by what he can't do but with gratitude for what he can do. I see death as a final step home for those who have struggled with life too long."

Anna responded, "Thanks, Emily, for making my day brighter. I needed your encouragement."

Anna entered Uncle Marv's room and glanced at the saying for the day on his door:

"If you think growing old is unpleasant, consider the alternative."

Uncle Marv was hunched over his computer working on genealogy searches when Anna entered. He had a serious look on his face, which was his default countenance. When he saw Anna, he straightened up his six-foot four-inch frame in his wheelchair and smiled broadly at her. "Anna, my dear, here you are! When you phoned this morning, I knew this would be a great day, especially since you've come to discuss the passion of my life – genealogy."

Anna settled in the lounge chair by the north wall of the room, and Uncle Marv maneuvered his wheelchair to face her. Beyond small talk, Anna updated Uncle Marv with the details of the Eldridge Gant murder, which he had just read about that morning as the feature story in the weekly *Wright County Journal*.

"Well, Anna, let's tackle this genealogical mystery. After your call, I dug out my Gertrude Ackerman file, and here it is. Almost all the information I have on your great grandmother Gertrude and Jakob Meyer is in this file folder. There are a few pieces from my Anton Schaar file which I also gathered, and here they are.

"Your murder case sounds fascinating, especially the Civil War coins part of it. I can't figure out, though, how Jakob would have possessed that much money, given that he was most likely a poor farmer.

"Perhaps I can shed some light on the lineage of three families that may help in your quest to determine who the coins belong to. But I have to warn you, I hit enough brick walls in my research that you'll have plenty of detective work to do. I would suggest you find someone who knows their way around genealogy because you don't have the background or experience to know where to look." Anna smiled; she had learned to enjoy his bluntness.

I have observed over many years that bluntness seems to be a trait of people of German descent; in any event it is a trait of Uncle Marv's. He is as upbeat a person as I've ever seen, given an incapacitating affliction that is gradually worsening, but I respect his down-to-earth telling it the way it is, without the hint of a smile.

However, when Anna smiled, Uncle Marv laughed, as if he knew he was being too stern. "Genealogy is something very wild and unpredictable, Anna; there are many rabbit trails. I once stumbled upon your great uncle Adolph's headstone in the St. George Cemetery near New Ulm while researching another family in my lineage. I was so excited I could hardly breathe for a few minutes. Genealogy is like creating a detective mystery of your own – putting together all the aspects of it. It's a challenge I have pursued since 1980 when I took a course on genealogy at North Hennepin Community College and was hooked for good.

"We are related because your great-grandmother was the child of my great-grandfather Anton by a second marriage…or so I thought. It took me until ten years ago to get into the branch of the Schaars who descended from that second marriage, and that's when I ran into a big surprise at the History Center in St Paul. The things that really mess up a clean genealogy are divorces, bigamists, second or third marriages, and illegitimate children.

"From 1865 to 1905, there was a Minnesota state census every ten years.

"I began with the August 13, 1870, national census figures. Look at this page I photocopied. My great-grandfather Anton is 49, but my great-grandmother Barbara is not listed as his wife, having been replaced by a woman named Elizabeth. I was unaware that Anton had a second wife before that. As you can see on the census sheet, my grandfather Joseph and his brothers and sisters by Barbara follow Elizabeth, and then comes Gertrude, three years old, and Adolph, two. I later found that Gertrude was born in January, so that would mean she was born in 1867 by this sheet.

"I then went back to the 1860 national census and the 1865 state census and found Barbara in both places. So she died somewhere between 1865 and 1870. I checked the local Catholic cemeteries near Medina to find her grave. I didn't have to look far. Her tombstone was in Holy Name Cemetery in Medina, with a date of death of 1865. I later found in my mother's scrapbook that the actual date of Barbara's death was June 14, 1865. Coincidentally, Jakob Meyer was discovered dead in his wood storage bin May 24, 1865, by his wife Elizabeth. This is the same Elizabeth that married Anton Schaar August 12, 1865, just three months after Jakob's death and two months after Barbara's death. Take a look at this marriage certificate from the District Court for the County of Hennepin, showing that Anton Schaar married Elizabeth Meyer and by oath declared that there were no legal impediments thereof. I photocopied it from microfilm at the History Center."

Anna had a surprised look on her face. "Uncle Marv, wasn't that a bit quick for Anton to marry Elizabeth?"

"Not at that time," answered Uncle Marv. "It happened all the time. Anton needed someone to raise his children and Elizabeth needed someone who had money coming in to provide for her basic needs. Sometimes such a marriage would occur within a couple of weeks. A long courtship was not one of the ingredients of these arrangements."

Anna had been writing feverishly in her notebook. "Uncle Marv, would you be willing to loan me that file so I can copy the pages and cut down on the amount of notes I need to take. I can't keep up?"

"Of course," replied Uncle Marv. Then his trademark generous smile moved his moustache up one-half inch on the edges. "I thought you'd be treading in deep water about this time, so I prepared a summary of how Gertrude could be the offspring of either Anton Schaar, my great-grandfather, or Jakob Meyer. See what you think," as he handed a sheet of paper to her.

Just then a nurse came into the room to take Uncle Marv's blood sugar count, which gave Anna a chance to look over the chart. Uncle Marv was diabetic. He kidded the nurse about just wanting to see him bleed and chit chatted with her about this and that. "Not bad," she said, after she read the blood sugar monitor and showed it to Uncle Marv. Then she turned to Anna, "How are you doing Anna? Are you involved in that horrible murder in Rockford last Monday?"

"That I am," replied Anna, with a smile and a wink.

Anna had a quick mind, but genealogy is a science in itself. She looked and looked at the chart, with a furrowed brow and eyes that said, "This is tough."

It's altogether important to study the dates above and the following chart to make heads or tails out of this mystery.

Anton Schaar b.1821, d.1893

> *m. Barbara Schmidt 1856 in New York, d. June 14, 1865*
>
> > *- Joseph Schaar b. 1857 and the rest of his siblings by this marriage*
>
> *m. Elizabeth Meyer August 12, 1865*
>
> > *- Gertrude Schaar if born in January 1867 or 1868*
> >
> > *- Adolph Schaar b. 1868, d. 1939, never married and no children*
> >
> > *- Helena Schaar b. 1870, d. 1958*
> >
> > *- Lewis Schaar b. 1884, d. 1971*

Jakob Meyer b.1832, d. May 24, 1865

> *m. Rebecca Jane Griffin 1850 in Boston, d. 1880 in insane asylum in Maine*
>
> > *- Eva Meyer 1851*
>
> *m. Elizabeth Kohler January 16, 1861, in Franklin Township, Minnesota*
>
> > *- Daniel Meyer b. December 1861, who shows up on the Schaar census in 1870 and 1875 but gone in the 1880 census, so died between 11 and 16 years of age*
> >
> > *- Gertrude Meyer if born in January 1866 but called Gertrude Schaar when Anton married her mother Elizabeth*

As the nurse left, Anna said to Uncle Marv, "This helps greatly, but I can't say that I fully understand it. There is some information you haven't covered yet, I think."

Uncle Marv smiled broadly at Anna and proceeded with the genealogy. "Be patient, Anna, I don't always go in straight lines. I'll eventually cover everything.

"Now, here comes the interesting part. The May 1, 1875, state census shows Gertrude as nine and Adolph as seven. That would mean Gertrude was born in 1866 and Adolph in 1868. On a form to recover Jakob Meyer's pension, which is another story in itself, Gertrude listed her birthday as January 21, 1866. "When Gertrude died in 1943, her daughter Anna Ackerman Fitzgerald listed her mother's birthdate as January 21, 1868, on a Minnesota State Department of Health 'Certificate of Death.'

"There must have been confusion on the part of her daughter about her mother's birthdate, because she listed Jakob Meyer as Gertrude's father. I searched newspapers at that time and found she was buried in St. Mary's Cemetery in South Minneapolis. I went there and found the dates on her tombstone as 1866 – 1943. I checked the obituaries and her birth date was not given."

Anna looked puzzled. "What does all this mean, Uncle Marv? I've been taking notes and I'll look over all the documents in your file later, but I can't get my mind around all the information."

Uncle Marv chuckled and then laughed out loud. "I thought that would happen, Anna, so I kept a genealogy chart until now that should help you visually see all the information. I researched the descendants of Gertrude Ackerman because I thought she was a Schaar. Now I'm not so sure. In fact, if I had to make a judgment, I'd say she was a Meyer, which would mean you and I are not related."

"Even if that's the case, you would still be Uncle Marv. I'm not about to give you up."

"I was hoping you would say that, Anna. I don't want to give you up either. Here's the chart."

Uncle Marv had a way of simplifying genealogy charts so Anna could understand them. His original genealogy charts are much more complicated, tracing each child of a marriage to the present time. Anna would have been completely lost trying to decipher a complete genealogy.

1. Jakob Meyer

   m. Elizabeth Kohler
   January 16, 1861

      2. Daniel Meyer b. 1861,
       d. 1875-1880

1. Anton Schaar

   m. Elizabeth Meyer
   August 12, 1865

      2. Gertrude Schaar
       b.1867/1868

2. Gertrude Meyer b. January 1866, eight months after Jakob's death and five months after Anton's marriage to Elizabeth

   m. Christian Ackerman May 31, 1880 (the chart is the same from here on)

      3. Olga Ackerman 1884, died of typhus in 1894

      3. John Ackerman 1888, died at childbirth

      3. Anna Ackerman 1896

        m. Michael Fitzgerald 1926

          4. Patrick Fitzgerald 1935, died 1937 of pneumonia

          4. Catherine Fitzgerald 1929, never married

          4. William Fitzgerald 1931

            m. Maggie McGrath 1964

            5. Anna Fitzgerald February 4, 1972

Uncle Marv cleared his throat and was about to impart some more facts, when a nurse came in with his medication for the morning. That gave Anna a chance to look over the latest chart. Uncle Marv bantered with the nurse about the falling snow. He said it was beautiful; she said it was too early and meant a long winter. Uncle Marv said the only part of winter he didn't like was that the open-air courtyard critters were gone until next spring – chickens, ducks, rabbits, and some pheasants – that served as a lively distraction for the residents.

When the nurse left, Anna expressed to Uncle Marv, "I've noticed you are always friendly with whoever comes into your room. I like that."

Uncle Marv answered in his serious tone again, "It's easy to be friendly because they are a terrific staff. This is a great care center. The only problem here is when my friends die, and that happens almost weekly. I have become acquainted with many people here over four years. It makes my life joyful while they're alive, but I become very sad when they die.

"A friend down the hall has been dying of cancer. He seemed to be doing quite well, and then he up and died yesterday. He didn't want to live anymore with all the pain. It's like he willed himself to die."

A man visiting another resident stopped by Marv's door and waved. Marv put on a big smile and waved back to him. It seemed everyone knew Marv – staff, residents, and visitors. And everyone loved Marv as if he were family to them. Anna had to put up with a constant interruption of people waving to Marv as they passed his door, but she didn't seem to mind.

Uncle Marv continued his narrative. "If Gertrude was born January 21, 1866, and I think that's the right date, then she would have been conceived sometime in April of 1865, when Elizabeth was married to Jakob Meyer and Barbara was married to Anton Schaar. I doubt that Anton even knew who Elizabeth was at the time.

"Another corroborating fact to Gertrude being born in 1866: she would have been fourteen when she married Christian Ackerman. That's young but was acceptable at the time. But if she were born in 1868, the other most likely date, she would have been twelve when she married, and that was not an acceptable age."

Just then the phone rang. It was Uncle Marv's nephew from Maple Grove who was making plans to visit Uncle Marv next week. The conversation lasted about five minutes. During that time Anna was studying the second chart with obvious interest.

When Uncle Marv put the phone down, Anna gasped. "As I ponder this chart, I think I realize something for the first time.

"If my great-grandmother Gertrude is a Meyer, as you think she is, then I am her only descendent. That would mean I'm the rightful heir to the Civil War coins in the tin box we have in our evidence room."

"Not quite so fast Anna. There are two impediments to that. You need to put the first chart I gave you alongside the second one, and I'll cover the additional information you should know. Then you'll see the whole picture.

"Let's look at the first chart. Jakob had a daughter by his first wife Rebecca Jane Griffin. They were married in 1850 and Eva Jennie Meyer was born in 1851; she married Alexander Gant in 1867."

"Gant?" Anna almost shouted.

Uncle Marv smiled broadly again. "Does that name sound familiar? I had no reason to follow that lineage further because Eva was definitely a Meyer, not a Schaar. Who knows how many descendants there are from Eva and how that would affect the claims on the Civil War coins? Apparently, Eldridge never thought about that when he figured the money was his. At this point, all Eva's descendants would have some sort of claim to 50% of the coins. You, as the only descendent of Gertrude, would have claim to the other 50%.

"Evidently Eva and Alexander Gant obtained a deed to Jakob's house and moved into it, and somehow the house was passed down through the years until Eldridge became the owner. There would be probate records if you wanted to pursue the trail to see if Eldridge indeed was deeded the house, which I expect he was. If Eldridge had a will, that's who the house would belong to, but the coins would be a different matter, given all the descendants there may have been between Eva and Eldridge. Even if he put the coins in his will, there could be challenges to that if his ancestors' children of the present day knew about the coins, which they probably wouldn't have except for Eldridge's murder and your involvement in the case. If he didn't have a will, the courts would have to decide who had a claim to the house and who had a claim to the coins. As I just mentioned, if your great-grandmother Gertrude was a Meyer instead of a Schaar, you would have a 50% share of the coins."

"Well, that becomes a 50% devaluing," said Anna matter of factly. Then her face brightened. "Aha," she exclaimed to Uncle Marv. "There may be a clue to the murder case here. Eldridge probably thought the coins were his alone because they were in his house. If Eldridge revealed the tin box to his heir, that person could wait until Eldridge died, being that he was 96. But if that heir told someone else about the tin box, without telling them where it was, then that someone else could be the mastermind behind the murder. I'm actually more interested in the murder case than any possibility of the coins belonging to me. I'm well enough off; I don't want to have greed creep into my life."

Anna's speculation about the tin box was not fanciful. She was always laying out what the possibilities were of any case, and she had an uncanny instinct to see clearly what others would never even think about. That's what made her a great detective.

By the conversation up until now, Anna would be thinking she had a 50% share of the Civil War coins. But I know what Uncle Marv knows, and I expect he is about to drop a bombshell on Anna that will knock her off her moorings.

"Don't give up 50% so easily yet, Anna. Gertrude obviously knew about Eva because both of them had been attempting to obtain Jakob Meyer's Civil War pension, and Eva won; she was awarded a benefit of $28 a month on November 27, 1896. Here's that document. But Gertrude did not stop fighting for the pension and kept writing letters to the Bureau of Pensions. Finally, on February 2, 1905, both of them were deposed by a Special Examiner of the Bureau of Pensions. I have photocopies here of both depositions from the National Archives in Washington D.C. Gertrude's claim was that Eva was conceived by Charles Gravely and Rebecca Jane Griffin prior to her marriage to Jakob Meyer, which meant she was illegitimate and Gertrude was the only descendent of Jakob 's. However, Gertrude could offer no proof of her claim, so Eva remained the recipient of the pension. As late as 1934, Gertrude wrote a letter to President Franklin D. Roosevelt on April 19, requesting her rightful pension. Here's a copy of that letter. We genealogists are an obsessed people, and I would have definitely researched whether Eva was illegitimate because of my built-in inquisitiveness, even though she wasn't a Schaar, except my muscular dystrophy did not allow me to go to Boston, where the answer probably lies. Also, by that time, I was convinced Gertrude was not a Schaar, but I had already charted out her genealogy before I reckoned that."

"So that's something for me to research, with the help of someone who knows their way around genealogy," said Anna with a smile, referring back to Uncle Marv's previous blunt statement. "But you said there were two impediments. What's the second one?"

Marv handed her a letter dated May 1, 1934, that was a response from an administrator assigned to answer Gertrude's letter to the President, after an investigation on his part of the matter. Anna read the letter silently and then the key part of it out loud.

> "After having been given the benefit of a thorough and exhaustive special examination at an added expense to this office, on the ground that if you were the child of the soldier at all you were illegitimate, as the marriage of the soldier to your mother was illegal and void by reason of the fact that he had a lawful undivorced wife at the time, which wife did not die until August 4, 1880, and for the further reason that it was not conclusively proved that you were a daughter of the soldier.
>
> Dr. G.M. Mittlain
> Chief of Contact
> For the Administration"

Anna's eyes opened wide. "It seems I just went from a 50% share to nothing," remarked Anna with a dazed look on her face, like a flood victim being interviewed on television.

I believed Anna when she said she was more interested in the murder than the money and that she didn't want greed to have a grasp on her life. But the last half hour had been a roller coaster in which she had thought she was the sole heir to the tin-box fortune, then the owner of a 50% share, and now nothing.

"You didn't tell me that Jakob never divorced his first wife, Uncle Marv."

"I did warn you, though, that I don't always go in a straight line. We genealogists like to cover our findings in our own way. Be patient until I finish. It's not as cut and dried as it seems." Anna was not patient. "Even if Eva were illegitimate, this letter eliminates me from consideration. That really throws things up in the air. If Eva isn't an heir, and I'm not an heir, where does that lead, Uncle Marv?"

"Into never-never land I'm afraid. You don't want to go there if you can avoid it; it could be done but it would be a phenomenal job. On the other hand, I've found that records were not always easy to find back in the mid-1800s. Stating that Jakob had not divorced his first wife doesn't make it a fact. Did the investigation only cover Augusta, Maine, where Jakob's first wife was in an insane asylum, or did it only cover Boston where Jakob lived? And what about the marriage license of Jakob and Elizabeth that I showed you, signed by Rev. Henry Singenstree stating there were no legal impediments to the marriage. Certainly an undivorced wife would be an impediment. Either Jakob lied under oath, or he presented the minister with a document showing he had divorced Rebecca, or he stated such as a fact under oath. This was a different era of time. Even reprobates like Jakob were not inclined to lie under oath."

"Something else for me to research," laughed Anna with more exasperation than humor.

"There's much work required to investigate the lineage of Gertrude Ackerman and Eva, and the marital status of Jakob before he married Elizabeth, to find out who the Civil War coins belong to, if anyone. That's my job as a detective, until I would find out I'm an heir; then I would be confronted with a conflict-of-interest scenario."

"I'm sorry I can't be of more help to you, Anna. I'm too far down the path of muscular dystrophy to be able to accomplish the significant genealogy work demanded to break through the brick walls. How about your old boyfriend Jack Quinn? When he used to come with you to visit me, I easily concluded he was more advanced in genealogy than I. Are the two of you on speaking terms?"

"Yes, Uncle Marv, we are on speaking terms. I was thinking of him when you mentioned I needed someone who knew his way around genealogy. I'll call him and see if he might be interested in helping out on this case."

"May I offer you a suggestion, Anna, to simplify your search? Focus on Eva being illegitimate or not, first, and on Jakob having divorced Rebecca or not, second, before you put in all the time to determine Eva's lineage down to the present day. That would be a monumental task. What you want to achieve is to make the complex simple."

Marv looked at his watch. "It's time for me to wheel over to the dining room for lunch."

"And it's time for me to get back to the office to prepare for tomorrow morning's team meeting. Thanks, Uncle Marv, for all your help."

Anna gave her uncle a big hug and a kiss, and went down the hall and out the door. When she reached her car, she opened the door, stood there a moment, and said out loud, "What an opportunity to get my love life back in order, as Gramma McGrath suggested, or rather demanded of me. I now have a reason to call Jack Quinn, the master genealogist, and we can spend many hours researching this case. He'll love it." Anna had a mischievous smile on her face, got in her car, and slammed the door as an exclamation mark.

CHAPTER FIVE

FRIDAY MORNING'S TEAM MEETING

Winter showed up early, Friday morning, October 20, with more snow and a biting wind. Anna wore a winter coat as she crossed the street to the Minneapolis Grain Exchange, entered the building, and rushed across the green marble floor on the way to the elevators. The downtown traffic had slowed her down, causing her to be late for the 9 a.m. team meeting.

All four team members were in the conference room when Anna arrived at 9:10. Before she had a chance to explain why she was late, Michael O'Hara cut her off. "Anna Fitzgerald! Just because you're Irish doesn't mean you can saunter in any time you feel like it." Anna's agitated demeanor vanished in an instant, was replaced by a smile, and then a laugh.

"I'm glad I made your day brighter, Michael, by giving you an opportunity to get back at me for my remark to you last Tuesday."

"And for that I thank you immensely," muttered Michael, trying to stifle his glee.

"Let's review our list from last Tuesday," said Anna, still smiling from Michael's rebuke.

Each had a list of 22 investigation action items that Anna had e-mailed to them. The meeting lasted nearly three hours, so I'll only cover the highlights that shed the most light on Eldridge Gant's murder.

Joe Wilshire, Sylvia Johnson, and Tony Talridge had spent the last three days interviewing neighbors and relatives.

Tony reported, "I interviewed, Eldridge's nephew, Lucius Gant, who is also a neighbor. It was a short visit. He told me he knew no reason why anyone would want to murder his uncle. It was like pulling teeth to get anything else out of him. But something in me said Lucius

51

was hiding vital information. After 20 years of investigative experience, I have learned to know when someone is holding back."

"Did any of you four discover any other relatives of Eldridge's?" asked Anna.

Joe answered that question. "I found a family history in a Bible in Eldridge's house that showed him as having one brother who died 14 years ago, and that brother had one child – Lucius. Those neighbors who knew Eldridge the best corroborated that information from what he had told them any number of times."

"Why don't I question Lucius in our interrogation room next week?" offered Anna. "Maybe a change in scenery will help loosen his memory."

"There is something else you should know before you question him," advanced Sylvia. "I didn't obtain any useful information in searching Mack and Toby's apartment, talking to their neighbors, or questioning their relatives and friends. The friends were in short supply. Mack and Toby were a couple of loners who kept to themselves; even their relatives were not familiar with what either of them was up to, but they didn't seem surprised when I acquainted them with Mack's and Toby's part in the murder of Eldridge Gant.

"However." Sylvia paused dramatically for suspense. "However, when I checked the cell phone records of Toby, I hit a bonanza. There were multiple calls between him and a Jimmy Gant, who I later discovered was one of two sons born to Lucius. The other we already know – Jacob Gant, the lawyer for Mack and Toby."

"That *is* a bonanza!" affirmed Anna. "Were there any calls between Mack and Jimmy Gant?"

"None," replied Sylvia, and a silence followed.

Anna broke the silence. "I visited Uncle Marv yesterday in Buffalo, and he covered with me the complexities of the lineage of Jakob Meyer." Anna filled them in on all the genealogical details of the conversation that had transpired between her and Uncle Marv, as well as she could remember them. "So I either have a 50% stake in the coins in Eldridge's house, a 100% claim, or nothing. But it may not make any difference to me personally. Uncle Marv shared with me that Jakob Meyer was a scoundrel and confirmed my suspicions that the Civil War coins in the tin box may have been obtained dishonestly.

That will be a major focus of my investigation, and if my suspicions are true, then I would want no part of the proceeds of the tin box. I am planning to contact my old boyfriend, Jack Quinn – you all know him – because he is an expert in genealogy. I want to ask you again, are you comfortable with my continuing with the genealogical search of who the money belongs to, given that part or all of it may belong to me?

Michael O'Hara spoke for the group. "We don't feel there is a conflict of interest yet, with so many questions to be answered, and especially with your statement that you may not want any of the money. None of us know what role Eva had in this or whether Gertrude was even a legitimate daughter of Jakob Meyer. When you find that out, we'll talk again. In the meantime, I'd suggest you run all this by our supervisor and see what he has to say." Anna said she was already planning on doing that but wanted to explain things to the team first.

Just as Anna and her team of four others were making good headway with the Eldridge Gant murder, a rash of criminal activities in Hennepin County meant they were all assigned to different teams for an embezzlement, a missing child, a suspected arson case, and various domestic assaults. It was rare when any detective was only assigned one case. So it took Anna a couple of weeks before interrogating Lucius Gant; she needed to give the team time to conduct a more thorough investigation of Lucius and his two sons, and they had to fit that in amongst their other responsibilities. There was an avalanche of information about Jimmy, all of it bad. He had been in scrapes with the law since he was twelve, and his criminal activities became more sophisticated as he grew older. He was now thirty-one and a drinker, a fighter, and otherwise nasty person. The police were trying to pin drug trafficking charges on him, but his older brother Jacob, the lawyer, had been able to keep Jimmy out of jail for the last ten years.

Holding Jimmy's rap sheet in front of her, Anna remarked to Sylvia, "Our friend Jimmy is a real son-of-a-bitch. Pardon my language, but that's the only term that seems to fit here." Sylvia nodded her head in agreement. "I wouldn't want to meet him in a dark alley, that's for sure."

Anna left the meeting and walked hurriedly down the hallway to talk to her supervisor. After she explained what she had covered with her team and their response, including Joe's definition of conflict of interest, he said he agreed with them but warned Anna that she needed to be very careful about this. "Once you find out about Eva and Gertrude, come and talk to me again. Then we'll know whether you have a conflict of interest or not. Right now, you are the one who can get the genealogy information the fastest. The alternative would be to hire a firm to do the investigation, and that would take much more time, not to mention a financial burden on the department."

The next day, Anna picked up Lucius at his home and brought him to the Grain Exchange Building, sixth floor, and ushered him into the interrogation room. The comfort of his home was gone, and Lucius had beads of sweat on his forehead. Anna's piercing stare made him feel even more uncomfortable.

Anna read him his Miranda rights. He had a blank look as if the information was lost on him. "Well, Lucius, it's time for you to become more cooperative in helping us solve the murder of your uncle." Lucius was anxious, but did not respond to her opening statement.

"I want to inform you that our investigation has uncovered much information, so your not being cooperative may make you eligible for an obstructing justice charge. Do you understand?"

That was plain language. Lucius nodded that he understood. He could have asked for a lawyer at this point, but as I said earlier, he was not gifted with much intellectual capacity and additionally was confused and anxious. The questioning continued.

"Are you the heir to Eldridge's assets?"

"I'm not sure what you mean," answered Lucius.

"Did Eldridge name you in his will to inherit everything he owns?"

Lucius looked around the room, apparently trying to figure out if Anna already knew this information. He must have concluded she did, even though she didn't, and answered, "Yes."

"Did Eldridge tell you that you were in his will?" Lucius nodded his head yes.

"Did Eldridge tell you about the tin box hidden under the floor in his bedroom?" Lucius again hesitated and answered, "No."

"Are you sure about that, Lucius? Remember the obstructing justice we can charge you with." Anna was an aggressive and creative investigator. She gave the impression that she already knew something even if she didn't. Her piercing eyes caused Lucius to crumble.

Lucius opened up. "Er, a... b...bout ten years ago, Eldridge found a n...note in a book in his library that had an entry written by his g...great-grandfather telling of the t...tin box and where it was hidden in the house. He showed me the book with the writing and pointed out the fl...floorboard in his bedroom where the b...box was hidden. He pledged me to secrecy and revealed I was n...named in his will to inherit everything he owned."

Anna quickly asked a follow-up question. "What was the name of the book, Lucius?"

"I don't r...remember, said Lucius. I th...think it was a b...blue book and was about wars."

The beads of sweat on Lucius' face turned into a torrent. "You d...don't think I had him murdered for the money, do you? Wouldn't I have d...done that right away if I were going to do it? And I knew I would eventually inherit the money anyway, though it wasn't really that much - $1,450 in g...gold and silver coins." Anna looked at him in disbelief, as if to say, "You aren't that dumb are you? Those coins are worth a fortune."

Anna responded to Lucius' question. "I'm not sure. I've more investigating to do before I say whether I think you were implicated or not. Did you tell anyone that you knew Eldridge had a tin box full of Civil War coins in his bedroom?"

Lucius' eyes opened wide at this question, and he put his hands over his face. He looked like a wild animal that had just been trapped, and he simply sat there saying nothing.

"Lucius, in our investigation of your uncle's murder, we obtained the call history of one of the killers' cell phones. There were 22 calls between your son Jimmy and a man named Toby, who is presently sitting in jail for the murder of your uncle. These calls were made in September and October of this year. Did you tell Jimmy about the tin box?"

Anna paused, as if she had more information; Lucius looked like he was pushed in a corner and had no place to go. With fear in his voice, Lucius broke the silence.

"L...last month I was h...having a few drinks with Jimmy, and I drank m...more than I usually do," stammered Lucius. "He asked me how Uncle Eldridge was getting along, and I foo...foolishly told him about the tin box with 150 gold and silver Civil War coins in it." Lucius ceased stammering once the gate had been opened.

"What made me tell him that I don't know? I had kept the secret ten years. I think the alcohol confused me. As soon as I gave him the information, I knew I had done wrong. Jimmy jumped on me to tell him where the tin box was. I lied to him and said I didn't know. Then I went to bed but didn't sleep the whole night. I was ashamed of myself. I was afraid Jimmy might do something rash, and it looks like he did. Can I go home now?" Lucius had tears in his eyes.

"I'll find a deputy to take you home," said Anna, "but I will be talking more to you later."

Later that evening, Anna recorded in her journal, "Today was a good day. I think I now know who the mastermind was behind the murder of Eldridge Gant. I felt sorry for Lucius when he had tears in his eyes after implicating his son as the one who hired Toby and Mack. It must be hard for a father to give up a son, even one as despicable as Jimmy. I can't blame Lucius for the way Jimmy grew up; he didn't have the mental horsepower to have reigned in such a renegade."

As Anna penned the last sentence, there were tears in her eyes, as she said out loud the last thing Lucius cried out as he was leaving the interrogation room. "Oh Jimmy, Jimmy, what have I done to you? I pray you are somehow innocent of this."

With all my experience of the highs and lows of the human race, I am rarely emotional, but there are times. Yes, there are times. I had tears in my eyes also, but not for the same reason as Anna. I remembered back some 3,000 years when King David was torn with remorse over the death of his son Absalom, even though Absalom had tried to take over his throne. When he was told Absalom was dead, he was shaken and went up to his room and wept. "O my son Absalom!

My son, my son Absalom! If only I had died instead of you – O Absalom, my son, my son!" I loved David, and I was frozen in my tracks when he lamented over a treacherous son who wanted to kill him. What a father! What a man! There have not been many like him throughout history. Truly he was a man after God's own heart.

The next morning, November 7, the sun was bright in the sky and the temperature was 51 degrees. All the snow of October was absorbed back into the air. It was fall again. Anna mobilized her team and filled them in on her discussion with Lucius the day before.

"Our one focus now is to find Jimmy Gant and question him, while we search for other evidence to arrest him for hiring the murder of Eldridge Gant. Michael and I will bring in Jimmy. The rest of you team up, get a warrant to search his house, and talk to as many people as you can until something turns up to tie him into the murder."

Well, saying you are going to bring Jimmy in and actually accomplishing it are two different things. Anna and Michael soon found that Jimmy had disappeared on or about October 10, and no one seemed to know where he had vanished. All their efforts to locate him – using notification to law enforcement agencies throughout the United States, checking the passenger lists of airplanes leaving Minneapolis about that time, and all the electronic technology available to them to find missing persons – turned up blank.

Joe, Sylvia, and Tony had more luck. They were able to convince a judge to issue a search warrant for Jimmy's house, and there they found a blank notepad on his desk that looked less than pristine. In the last few pages of the notepad were notes of Jimmy's conversations with Toby that without a doubt tied him into hiring Toby and Mack to force Eldridge to tell them where the tin box was, even if they had to torture him. It was not like Jimmy to have left such evidence that was so incriminating. There was a reason why he was so careless, but we'll let that unfold in Anna's discovery timeline.

This time Tony called for a team meeting. "Do you think this will be evidence enough to arrest Jimmy?" Tony asked Anna as he handed her a copy of the notes. "I brought the original to the crime lab, and

Jimmy's fingerprints were all over the pad and the pen that was used to write the notes."

"Wow! Great work guys," exclaimed Anna. "We now have all the evidence needed to arrest Jimmy, but, unfortunately, he has disappeared and we can't find him. We need to turn over every rock, follow every lead, and redouble our efforts with other government agencies. I wish we could talk to Toby and show him this evidence, but we can't do that without having Jacob Gant there, and I don't want him to know yet what we have. He's more likely to protect Jimmy than tell us where he is. He'd advise Jimmy to get out of the country, if Jimmy hasn't already done so. Let's find Jimmy!"

Anna had already called Jack Quinn for a date that very evening, enticing him with the genealogy search associated with the murder and asking for his help. Jack said, "I would be pleased to help you Anna," and as he hung up the phone with a twinkle in his eyes, he whispered "I wonder what she meant by, 'It will be good to see you again, Jack, and it will please my Gramma McGrath.'"

CHAPTER SIX

ANOTHER VISIT WITH UNCLE MARV

On the evening of November 14, the weather was still pretending to be fall. Anna and Jack's date was for 5:30 p.m. at Patrick McGovern's Pub on 7th Street in downtown St. Paul, not far from where Jack lived.

Jack arrived first and was shown to the booth he had requested in the main dining room, on the other side of a rather large bar area. This was their first real date in two years, though they had seen each other in courthouses in their professional capacities and had talked now and again on the phone over the past two years. I had to laugh watching Jack; he looked as if he were in the final stages of a nervous breakdown, pushing the silverware around the table, looking toward the door of the dining room as if he were expecting a gunman to come rushing through it, and sneaking furtive glances at his watch which had already passed 5:30. He mumbled to himself, "Where are you Anna? I'm waiting for you. Should I call her on her cell phone or not? I'll give her ten more minutes and then call; no, five more minutes."

Where indeed was Anna? How could she possibly be late for one of the most important dinners of her life? Well, Interstate 94 moves slowly at 5:00 p.m., but Anna had allowed for that. What she didn't allow for was a traffic accident on the eastbound lane that turned the interstate into a giant parking lot. Unlike the mumbling of Jack, Anna was practically screaming. "How could this happen on this day of all days? I was nervous enough already; now I'm at my wits end. What a way to meet after two years! I'm going to be late and Jack will immediately think it's because I was working and that he's still second fiddle. That's the last thing I wanted to happen."

Her watch read 5:40 when suddenly calm came over her. "I'll call Jack and let him know what's happening. He'll understand."

Just before Jack was about to call Anna, his phone rang and it was her. He seemed almost afraid to answer, as if something had come up at her job and she wouldn't be able to meet him at McGovern's. After five seconds of looking at Anna's name on his cell phone, he flipped it open and pressed the send button. He only had a chance to say hello before Anna took over the conversation. "Jack, I left work at 4:30 to arrive at McGovern's early, but there's been a terrible accident in front of me and no cars are moving until they get three wrecked cars off the road. Three ambulances have come in from the opposite direction, so I'm afraid there are serious injuries. "I want nothing more than to be there with you, but I'm afraid it may be 6:00 or later before I get there. Are you OK waiting?"

Jack breathed a sigh of relief, and his nervousness disappeared. "Anna, if it takes you until 7:00 to get here, I'll be waiting for you. I'm so relieved to hear from you and know what's happening."

Just then, the traffic started moving again, so they ended the phone conversation, and Anna was able to reach the restaurant by 5:55. She checked her face in the car mirror, made minor adjustments, straightened her hair and clothes, and headed in the front door where Jack was waiting for her.

After they were seated and their waiter had fetched them each a pint of Guinness, Anna put her right hand on top of Jack's left hand and smiled. It appeared as if an electric shock had traveled through Jack and rendered him speechless. Eventually, he smiled.

"Do you still have feelings for me, Jack, even though you've been so disappointed with me for putting my job first?"

"You know I do, Anna, but I'm still cautious of any relationship between us because of what you just said. I love my job, but I love you more. It needs to be the same way with you, or it won't work between us."

Anna then shared with Jack the conversation she had with Gramma McGrath a month ago, and her resolve to rearrange her job and her love life. "I wouldn't have called you, Jack, even though I need help with a genealogical mystery, if I were not ready to put you first in my life."

Jack put his other hand on top of hers and spoke as if the wind had been knocked out of him by a medicine ball thrown into his midsection. "Oh, Anna, I've never loved anyone but you. When you'd call me on the phone or when we met by chance in the Hennepin County Court House over the past two years, my heart rate would go up by twenty points. Are you proposing we start dating again and see what happens?"

"That's exactly what I'm proposing. But I want to be honest with you. I need a genealogy expert like you to help me solve a series of ancestry mysteries. I mischievously thought of you because this would be a way to spend time with you again; nothing else seemed to work to catch your attention. I also want to be honest with you about one other item. If there were not the matter of the genealogical mysteries, I'd still want to be with you tonight and build a relationship with you again."

Nothing more was spoken about genealogy that night. And in the period of a two-hour supper, they were sweethearts again. As they left the pub to head for their cars, Jack pulled Anna close to him and kissed her tenderly. This time it was Anna's turn to look like an electric shock had zapped her. Her body quivered, and she put her hands on Jack's face and kissed him more robustly than he had kissed her.

"Are you free this Saturday morning to visit Uncle Marv and discuss the case with him? You'll know the questions to ask that I didn't."

"It's a date," said Jack. "Are you free for the rest of Saturday for an extended date after we leave Marv?"

"I am," said Anna. "What are you intending we do?"

"We'll figure that out together when Saturday comes."

How joyful were those four days before they would meet again! Jack was friendlier to everyone than he had ever been before. And at appropriate and inappropriate times, he would stare off into space as if he were completely removed from his surroundings. I've seen the look he had on his face before; it's the look of a person in love.

Anna was also friendlier to her co-workers than any of them had seen before, and that secret smile that would light up her face at appropriate and inappropriate times was a wonder to behold. Anna also was in love.

At 9:30 on Saturday morning, Anna and Jack pulled into the parking lot of Park View Care Center. November was no longer pretending to be fall; light snow was falling, the temperature was 19 degrees, and the forecast was for a massive blizzard on Sunday.

Uncle Marv was in his usual position, hunched over his computer, when Anna and Jack arrived at his door. Marv lifted his head, straightened up in his wheel chair, and invited them in. "Anna, to what do I owe this pleasant surprise?" Then he smiled broadly with a playful tone in his voice. "Hello Jack, it's good to see you. I wonder if your presence here has anything to do with the genealogy discussion Anna and I had last month?"

Jack shook Marv's hand warmly and answered with an impish smile on his face. "Wrong guess, Marv. I'm here to ask for your niece's hand in marriage." Anna's face turned the color of her hair. Marv sat back in his chair with his eyebrows raised. There was silence for about fifteen seconds. Neither Anna nor Uncle Marv had the breath to utter any words.

Then Jack started laughing. "I'm just kidding the both of you, but one day I won't be. Yes, Marv, I'm here to engage in a discussion of matters of genealogy resulting from the murder of Eldridge Gant."

Anna settled into the same lounge chair against the north wall as her last visit and stared at Jack more than she looked to Uncle Marv. Jack sat on the bed against the west wall with a subtle smile and his eyes on Anna most of the time. Anna was still shaking her head from Jack's comment about asking for her hand. Apparently, she was used to Jack's prankish sense of humor and made no comment. After all, Jack was 100% Irish, and that always had to be taken into account.

Uncle Marv started with the genealogical overview. Jack quickly grasped the big picture and started asking Marv questions that Anna was not experienced enough to ask.

"Let's focus on the three big questions of this ancestral search," stated Jack, with the authority of one who knew what he was about.

"First, it seems from what you showed me, Marv, that Gertrude is a Meyer and not a Schaar. But that is guesswork. We need absolute proof of her birthdate. The date Gertrude gave for her birth in her communication with the Pension Bureau may be tainted by her desire to have received Alden's pension. The other dates are a mishmash of conflicting information. What church was Anton Schaar attending when Gertrude was born? The church records would have her baptism written down and her date of birth would also most likely be given. Or a family Bible perhaps."

Marv was ready for those two questions. "I found Barbara Schaar's tombstone in Holy Name Church in Medina. I have other family information that shows Anton attended Holy Name Church, but his tombstone was not there. I checked nearby Catholic Church cemeteries and found Anton's grave site at St. Peter and Paul's Church in Loretto, and he shows up in church records there in 1870."

"So we need to go over the church records of Holy Name Church in 1866, 1867, and 1868; but somehow I have a feeling, Marv, that you've already pursued that," said Jack.

"That's one of the first things I did," replied Marv. "On March 4, 1911, the rectory was burned to the ground by a faulty stove but quickly rebuilt, completed just before the church burned down on June 3, 1911, by a lightning strike. Tragedies seem to come in twos. It was assumed the church records were lost in the fire. I asked everyone I could think of if the records may have survived somehow. Every person I interviewed built the brick wall higher and thicker. The only information I did receive, and I don't remember exactly where, is that the church records at that time were very complete and accurate, all the way back to 1857, when church was held in the homes of various parishioners. Good church records are not always the case, as you know. The church was rebuilt after the fire and then rebuilt again after 1980, when I last saw it. You could try talking to the church folks there again, just in case something has turned up in the last twenty-five years.

"As to a family Bible, I received the Bible that would have been in Anton's house from my Aunt Gladys, but it was filled with inaccuracies and Gertrude's name was not even in it."

Anna had been silent this whole time, and seemingly decided she had something to offer.

"Jack, perhaps we should go to Holy Name Church and see if anything new has occurred about the records; it's right off Highway 55 on our way home." Jack nodded his head and started his next question.

"Second, we need to find if Eva is the legitimate daughter of Jakob Meyer or not. If she were his daughter, it seems strange that he didn't have anything to do with her once he put Rebecca in the insane asylum in Maine. What religion was Jakob, Marv?"

"Everyone in these various genealogies is Catholic," responded Marv, "Meyers, Schaars, and their wives and children. The only exception I know of is my great Uncle John, who became a Lutheran, but he's not involved in any lineage we're pursuing."

"You mentioned, Marv, that you would have gone to Boston and started searching there for a church record on Eva, but your health didn't permit it. What church would you have gone to?"

Marv shook his head. "That's another problem. I had no idea where to start. There must have been hundreds of Catholic churches in Boston at that time, and who knows how good their records were. I'm sorry I can't help you there."

"Hmm," said Jack, with a puzzled look on his face. "I'll need to check out when Massachusetts had births recorded and whether I can research that from here or need to go to Boston. If that's not productive, Anna and I need to do some research on likely churches Jakob might have belonged to, and then one of us needs to go to Boston to rummage around the likely churches. This could either be very easy or very tough."

Anna had a smile on her face. "It will be easier for you to take the time off work than me, Jack, my darling. Besides you are the genealogy guru here. You'd know how to look things up; I wouldn't have a clue."

Jack brightened at the word darling from Anna's lips, even though he must have known she used such language with many people, but there was a tone to the word that was different than what she used with someone like Michael O'Hara, for example. You have no idea what the words "my darling" mean until you hear how it is said and the look on the face of the person who says it. Anna said it with a smile and in a manner of endearment that was anything but facetious. "I guess you're right, Anna. But the two of us can research together what churches I should go to. Your detective skills will be most helpful."

Marv had been observing the interaction between Anna and Jack for some time now, and he decided it was time to acknowledge what he was seeing. "Personally, I had thought the task of sorting this genealogy out was hopeless, but you two make a great team, and I believe you'll have the answer to where Gertrude Ackerman came from within a few months."

It was time for Jack's third big question. "From the information you've given me, Marv, my gut tells me that Jakob divorced Rebecca somewhere before the time he left Boston. The divorce would have taken place in Boston, where Jakob was living, not in Augusta, Maine, where Rebecca was in the asylum. There apparently was no recorded certificate of the divorce in vital statistics, or the administrator who wrote the letter to Gertrude on the behalf of President Roosevelt would have found it. There are other ways to look for a recorded divorce that take more time than the administrator would have spent. It's worth investigating. I can do that when I'm in Boston."

Anna said there was something that had been bothering her more and more. "Uncle Marv, I've become increasingly concerned about where Jakob's money came from. I don't have a good feeling that it came to him honestly."

"I don't have a good feeling about that either, Anna. Let me tell you what I know that I have not already told you."

Uncle Marv was just about to start a story, but the conversation about genealogy came to an abrupt end, for just at that time a friend of Marv's named Ronald entered the door and went over to sit on the bed alongside Jack. Ronald was eighty-six-years old. If he had any sense he was interrupting a conversation, he didn't show it. He knew Anna from previous visits, but not Jack. "Well, who are you young man?" asked Ronald.

"I'm Anna's lover," said Jack. "I dare not let her out of my sight for a minute because I'm afraid she'll run off with another man. She's a flighty one, all right."

Ronald sat up as straight on the bed as a man eighty-six can sit; Uncle Marv and Anna were smiling and then laughing. Ronald didn't know what to say, so he started in with a litany of his ailments and problems. Marv was a good listener and encouraged Ronald that he needed to carry on no matter what situations or circumstances he found himself in. It's strange that a person could come from outside the care center and visit someone with a terminal affliction as dreadful as muscular dystrophy and tell about his own problems. I've seen that so often it doesn't surprise me anymore. One of the worst cases I viewed was a young man dying from a car accident, breathing heavily and in excruciating pain, awaiting his last breath, and his father was standing by him telling him about shoveling snow that morning, pulling a muscle in his back, and how painful that was. It's hard to believe. But maybe with Marv it served a purpose, since he was able to forget about his own health problems and sympathize with Ronald about his.

"Uncle Marv," said Anna, "Jack and I are going to leave now. My lover needs to take me out to lunch. We'll leave you in good hands with Ronald."

Marv asked, "Are you coming for my birthday next Saturday?" Anna said she was; Jack mentioned he wouldn't be able to because he'd be in Chicago until later that day. Marv then said, "I'll tell you a bit more about Jakob Meyer then."

Anna gave Uncle Marv a hug and a kiss and thanked him for all the information, as did Jack. On the way out the door, Jack put his hand on Anna's posterior as one parting shot for Ronald. He nearly fell off the bed. I had to laugh myself.

Anna and Jack stopped to eat at the Medina Ballroom, then went over to Holy Name Church to talk to the pastor about the lost church records. The snow was becoming heavier, so they questioned whether to venture into the graveyard to see Barbara Schaar's grave. Jack, the consummate genealogist, remarked with a face set in stone, "Of course we have to see Barbara's grave. We're here and she's there. We may not come back this way again."

Anna laughed. "If a blizzard doesn't bother you, it doesn't bother me. Let's do it." A graveyard covered by snow is not easy to navigate. Anna and Jack were laughing and holding on to each other to keep from falling, and they were rewarded with the tombstone of Barbara Schaar. They stood in front of the stone for a few minutes, and then headed for the rectory.

Father Jansen was in and had time to meet with them. He was well familiar with the lost church records of 1911. "That is a terrible thing to happen to a church," he said, "not to mention a terrible thing to happen to those whose genealogy search ends at my front door. The priest at the time survived the rectory fire, but died trying to save the sacraments in the church fire. It seemed to be well known that the records were kept in the church itself and not in the rectory; but in either event, the records would have been burned. I expect every search was conducted to find the records, but to no avail."

Anna gave Father Jansen her business card. "If any more information turns up about the church records, could you give me a call?" She had a look indicating that after nearly one hundred years, that was not likely to happen. Father Jansen had the same look on his face. But it had to be done. It was a routine for a detective.

"How would you like dinner at my flat?" Anna asked Jack as they left the rectory. "We can have a glass of wine and discuss what happened today and plot out a plan of discovery, and then maybe we could watch a movie I just received from Netflix."

Anna had a nice place in the warehouse district of downtown Minneapolis – a one-bedroom flat in Heritage Landing on 1st Street North. It had high ceilings, exposed duct work, a good-sized bedroom and a large "great room." The kitchen was small but very suitable for one person who did not often entertain. The decoration was very eclectic; few items of furniture or art matched anything else. Yet it had a character that was appealing to the eye. Against the east wall of the "great room" was a huge sofa that doubled as a hideabed. It was useful for those few times when Anna had visitors from out of town.

Anna and Jack sat on the couch, each with a glass of wine in hand. "Be honest with me, Jack, what are the chances that we'll be able to solve the mystery of whom the coins belong to?"

"I can't say what the chances are until we start the search. It will take a heap of work and a boatload of luck, but it is possible. What bothers me the most is what happened on the way back at Holy Name Church in Medina. The missing church records present a real problem. In legal terms, there is not much back then but church records. I can check for Bibles, journals, someone who viewed the church records and made note of what he saw, a manuscript of school records before Anna was seven, or maybe even a court case."

"What kind of a court case?" queried Anna.

Jack laughed. "Well, maybe I'll find in the Minneapolis paper of the time (I think it was called the Journal) that Jakob Meyer beat his wife Elizabeth in 1865 and that she was pregnant. A long shot for sure, but you just never know what might pop up in a genealogical search. I know there's an 1881 history book of Hennepin County that might give me the ages of Anton Schaar's children. And there are other sources I could check, like Ancestry.com. None of these, of course, are a sure thing."

Anna had a meditative look and then her face lit up. "You know, Jack, we don't have to have absolute, undisputable proof of parentage. We only need enough information to convince a judge to exhume the bodies of Jakob Meyer and Gertrude Ackerman to do a DNA match. If we present the information we have and positive DNA results, that should take care of the burden of proof. I'll check with our crime lab on how accurate DNA results would be from a body that has been in the ground for 141 years."

Jack clapped his hands. "We make a good team, Anna. I hadn't thought of the role DNA could play.

"The trip to Boston will be critical. Before I go there, I'll want to research from back here what repositories there are to look in – civil archives, the New England Historic Genealogical Society, local historical societies, libraries, and anything else that comes to mind. If nothing shows up there, I'll try to find where Jakob Meyer lived in Boston, and assume the church he and Rebecca attended would be nearby. I'm assuming because they were Catholic that they had Eva baptized. In those days, baptism happened within a couple weeks of a birth. Whatever there is to research, I'll research.

"The matter of the divorce will be another hit-or-miss situation. The only thing I can think to do there is to go to the Clerk of Court's office and wade through pages in day book ledgers, hoping to find an entry that somehow missed being recorded in vital statistics. I'll check the vital statistics first, which are easily researched, in case the administrator who wrote that letter to Gertrude Ackerman was sloppy."

Anna took a sip of her wine and responded to Jack. "Jack, my darling, it all sounds impossible. So many pieces have to come together. I don't see how it can be done. Is it worth even trying? It will take so much of your time; I'm concerned about that."

"Anna, genealogy isn't work to me. It's a passion. I love it and consider it my second career. Certainly, this is a challenge, but it's not as impossible as you may think. I've been involved in genealogy since I was sixteen years old, and I've learned to never say something isn't possible. Let's start down the path and then we can say what's possible and what's not."

Anna moved over to Jack, and he put his arm around her. She looked up in his face with a warm look that I hadn't seen on her face for more than two years. "Jack, what a fool I was to let you get away from me for two years. What a fool I was to consider my work more important than you. I'm not absorbed in your solving a genealogy mystery. I'm interested in you, more than who was the mastermind behind Eldridge Gant's murder and more than whom the box of Civil War coins belong to." And then she kissed him. Anna was always one to aggressively go after what she wanted.

Jack had tears in his eyes. "Oh, Anna, my sweetheart, I've loved you since that first date we had at Murray's restaurant four years ago. I knew then you were the only woman for me. I've had dates in the last two years, but no one could measure up to you. I've been praying hard that you'd eventually realize that a job is not something you want to build a life around. I've been waiting for you, Anna. And now here we are, picking up where we left off when we first dated. Are you really sure that our relationship is more important than your job?"

"Jack, my love, if you asked me to resign my position with the Hennepin County Investigative Division and work in a grocery store, I'd do it tomorrow. I wouldn't think it over or hesitate. That's what I'd do." She was dead serious.

Jack laughed. "I'd never ask you to give up your career and work in a grocery store. But your saying that is what I wanted to hear. You don't need to be dramatic. Just keep me first."

"I will, Jack, I will. There's no turning back for me. You are what I want first in my life." At that, Anna took Jack's wine glass out of his hand and placed it on the coffee table, along with her glass. Then she sat down as close to him as she could get and embraced him with a hug reserved only for those in love. I was going to say they sat like that for five minutes without saying anything, but I couldn't really say the position they were in was sitting. I really couldn't.

Anna finally extricated herself from the embrace and announced she was hungry and would fix a spaghetti dinner. Jack sat on the couch in a state of reverie, with a smile on his face, and a glow in his cheeks, as if to say, "I'm finally at peace."

After supper, they cleared the table together and put the dishes in the dishwasher; then sat and talked until midnight. They never did watch a movie. There was much catching up to do. As Jack got up to leave, Anna looked out the double windows on her deck facing 1st Street. "Jack, the storm has hit early. It's a raging blizzard out there. I don't want you to risk your life going home. You'll stay here tonight." And so he did.

CHAPTER SEVEN

ANNA QUESTIONS LUCIUS AGAIN

Anna connected with her team on November 21, but there was little progress in locating the main mover of the murder of Eldridge Gant, which in legal terms is called Conspiracy of Murder in the First Degree. The extensive effort to discover the whereabouts of Jimmy Gant was without results, as if he had vanished from the face of the earth. But I knew better. I knew where he was. I had confidence Anna's team would also find him, eventually.

Michael O'Hara advanced a hypothesis. "Perhaps we're not finding Jimmy because we're searching for him above ground. Perchance a rival dope ring decided to eliminate the competition, and he's now residing in a basement apartment, six feet underground."

Anna responded, "On a 'best for mankind' standpoint, I'd say that would be a good outcome. On a 'best for our investigation' standpoint, it would bring our 'conspiracy of murder' charge to a dead end." Anna laughed when she realized what she had just said. "I didn't mean to make that a pun; it just happened."

Tony Talridge, the veteran investigator, had advice. "I think it's time to question Lucius Gant again. I still don't think he's given us the whole story. I can't imagine he wouldn't know where his son was hiding."

Sylvia Johnson, the one who first questioned Mack and Toby, also had an opinion. "Let's question Jacob Gant. If he doesn't talk to us, we've lost nothing. However, if he knows Jimmy is dead, he wouldn't have to protect him. After all, he's the one intimately acquainted with the dope ring in which Jimmy is the number one and might know if there was a hit on Jimmy. It's worth a try."

Finally, Joe Wilshire put in his two cents worth. "I recommend we examine Jimmy's house again with extra-sharp eyes. If he was careless enough to leave the pad of paper on his desk with the last few pages that incriminated him, there may be other evidence he left behind that could lead us to where he went."

"You four are hitting on all cylinders," said Anna with unconcealed delight. "We make a fantastic team. Let's follow up on all suggestions.

"Tony, could you chat with Jacob Gant? You have a long history with him, and he respects you. Joe, would you and Sylvia turn Jimmy's house upside down and see what you can find? When I know the results of those two endeavors, I'll pay a visit to our friend Lucius and pull out of him whatever he's hiding. He's afraid of me, and I'll scare the hell out of him."

I become bored with monochromatic people. There are no surprises in them, and surprises bring color for me to the generally dreary landscape of this world. Anna can be so tender and compassionate with her family, friends, and co-workers; but she can also be as tough as nails with criminals.

Jacob Gant was in Los Angeles the week after Thanksgiving. Tony felt it was best to wait until he returned and made an appointment to meet him in his office on December 4. I listened to the conversation between them, which was cordial, but Jacob was not about to admit Jimmy was heading up a dope ring in Minneapolis and might have been bumped off. However, his voice gave evidence he was worried about Jimmy. He informed Tony curtly that Jimmy had not confided in him about leaving town or where he would be living. Tony had developed a sense over the years of when Jacob was lying and when he was telling the truth. In this case, he felt Jacob was telling the truth and reported such to the team. I knew he was right.

Sylvia and Joe scoured Jimmy's house for additional clues. They found clothes missing from the closets and personal items that a person would have in a bathroom, for example, all gone. The house was empty of suitcases. Valuables that a thief would have taken remained in the house. They concluded Jimmy had departed in a hurry and grabbed what he needed to live on for an extended period of time. As they left the house, Joe remarked to Sylvia, "It looks like Jimmy is living someplace above ground." There were no clues as to where that might be.

It was time for Anna to question Lucius.

Two days after Tony talked to Jacob, Anna drove from her office to Rockford and pulled into Lucius' driveway. When Lucius heard the car, he pulled back the curtain on the side window of the front door and saw Anna exit her black Impala. He scurried into his bedroom to hide, but Anna had seen him pull back the curtain. She rang the doorbell and stood there for a minute. No Lucius. Then she found the door was open, so she walked into the house and announced her presence. "This is Detective Fitzgerald, Lucius. I know you are here. Come out here so we can talk." The bedroom door opened and there was Lucius. Anna, with a voice that allowed for no disobedience, said, "Let's sit at the dining room table."

Anna opened the conversation without going for the throat right away. "How are you doing, Lucius?"

"Fine," he said warily.

"I warned you I'd be questioning you again one day. I chose your house this time," Anna said with a harsh bite to her words, "so you'd be less nervous and less likely to withhold information. I don't think you gave me the whole story last time. Let me remind you that in a murder case, an Obstructing Legal Process charge would be a felony, and you'd be facing jail time. I must caution you that we have more information on the murder of your uncle now and the implication of your son Jimmy, and I won't tolerate your holding information back."

Anna said that Lucius should be more comfortable in his own home, but her threatening monologue did anything but put Lucius at ease. He had that look of a trapped animal again.

Anna's voice was not friendly when she asked, "When is the last time you saw Jimmy?"

Lucius was silent for 15 seconds, but he could not escape the eyes of Anna staring right through him. "J...Jimmy came over to m...my house on October 10; I th...thought he had come to wish m...me happy birthday, but he announced th...that he was leaving town that night. Th...then he left, and I h...haven't seen him since."

Lucius had barely finished his last sentence when Anna served up the next one. "Where was he going, Lucius?"

"He d...didn't tell me. I s...swear he didn't tell me. I'm worried about him. H...he was very anxious."

"What else did he say?" Anna was now into a pattern of rapid-fire questions that didn't allow Lucius time to think, while she stared at him with those penetrating blue eyes.

"H...he just t...told me th...that he was in a troubling situation and n...needed to pick up his wife and daughter in Madison, Wisconsin, and take them somewhere to hide. He told me he w...wouldn't tell me where because then I wouldn't have to l...lie to whoever might ask me questions – like you."

I had heard the whole conversation between Jimmy and Lucius; and what Lucius said was true, but he left out considerable information. If Anna fails to find Jimmy and obtain his side of the conversation, I'll tell you what the full story was later. I always trust the truth will eventually appear, and I'm often disappointed when it doesn't. Mankind lives in a world of lies, deception, and hidden agendas.

"Lucius, did Jimmy tell you anything about his plans to have Eldridge murdered by a couple of thugs?"

"No, h...he said nothing about that. If he had, d...don't you think I would have done something to p...protect my uncle?" Now that was an outright lie, but Anna said she believed Lucius because he most certainly would have done something to protect his uncle had he known Jimmy's intentions. I was frustrated that Anna didn't dig deeper into this, but that's because I knew something that Anna didn't know. I can't really fault her.

Anna suddenly changed the direction of her questioning. "You disclosed to me a month ago there was a book in Eldridge's library with a note between chapters revealing where the Civil War coins were hidden. Let's walk over to Eldridge's house and find that book."

It was a short walk, which was beneficial, because the weather was five degrees above zero with a fifteen mile-per-hour wind. Lucius seemed much more at ease when Anna changed the focus of the questioning. I'd guess he did not want to go any further down the path Anna was heading, and it was a relief to him when she believed him. Anna did not yet have Tony Talridge's sense of when a person was lying to him; it comes with experience and time.

They ascended the steps from the first story to the second, turned left at the top of the stairs, and walked into the library, where Anna suspended the speechlessness of the last five minutes. "Where's the book, Lucius?" Lucius looked confused. "I don't know for sure."

"Which bookcase were you standing by with Eldridge?"

"I think the big one against the wall."

"And you say the color of the book was blue and had something to do with wars?"

"Yes."

Anna saw three blue books in the bookcase, but none of them was the right book. Then she started at the top shelf and worked her way down. On the third shelf from the top was a green book entitled *Fifteen Decisive Battles of the World*, by Sir Edward Creasy. She put on plastic gloves to protect all fingerprints and pulled out the book.

"Is this the book, Lucius?"

"I believe it is."

"Where is the note?"

"Between two chapters I think."

"What two chapters?"

"I don't know."

Anna started paging through the chapters but did not have to go far. There between the fourth and fifth chapters was the note. It was addressed to Elizabeth, Jakob's wife, explaining where the tin box was hidden, what was in it, and that it was Elizabeth's inheritance.

The rest of the note to Elizabeth startled Anna.

> I tradded most of $5000 in greenbacks I depossited in 3 St. Paul banks duren the war fer the brandy new gold and silver coins when I were mustered out of service at Fort Snelling on April 29, 1864. I did it for you, Elizabeth the coins are your's if anytheng happens to me.
> Jakob Meyer

This reinforced Anna's suspicions of the money not being honestly come by. Under her breath she said, "I'll need to do some research on how much money soldiers were paid in the Civil War." Lucius did not catch what she said because his hearing was less than adequate. Now if Anna was startled by the first note, she was astounded by a second note below the first. It was not addressed to Elizabeth, but it must have been meant for her eyes.

If you wanna know more about Eva pretend her a farmer and the
story is on page 440.

"What's this about, Lucius?" demanded Anna.

"I don't know who Eva is," answered Lucius, and Eldridge didn't
say anything about it, so I figured it had nothing to do with the money
or anything else." Well, it had a lot to do with the money, but
Eldridge's mind was not able to grasp the legalities of the matter, even
if he were told Eva was in his lineage.

Lucius may not have known who Eva was, but Anna certainly did
– she was Jakob Meyer's daughter from his first marriage to Rebecca
Jane Griffin. Anna quickly turned the pages to find 440, but there were
not 440 pages in *Fifteen Decisive Battles of the World*.

"Are you sure Eldridge didn't say anything about this note when
he showed you the page in the book we're looking at?" questioned
Anna with a tone to her voice that made Lucius visibly shudder.

"I can't remember him saying anything. I didn't ask any questions
and he didn't offer any information," answered Lucius.

Anna carefully placed the book in the evidence bag she had
brought with her to take to the crime lab and then to the sixth floor
evidence room. It had all happened so fast that Anna didn't have time
to react. She asked Lucius to go downstairs and wait for her, sat down
in a chair in the library, pulled the book out of the evidence bag,
opened it to the page of the note, and talked to the books. "This is
amazingly energizing. Here I am in 2006 reading a note in the
handwriting of who may be my great-great-grandfather in the year
1865. My eyes have just spanned 141 years of history. I can't explain
the feeling I have. It's exhilarating." She sat there for five minutes
looking at the note and being in a state of reverie, oblivious to Lucius
downstairs walking around and muttering to himself. Then she
reverently arose and went downstairs.

Anna and Lucius returned to his house, and Anna tried to trap him
any number of times into revealing where Jimmy was. She reminded
him of the Obstructing Legal Process charge and that Lucius would
spend time in prison. I know something about Lucius that in his mind
would consign the threat of going to prison as a death sentence; yet he
did not waver. He told Anna he absolutely did not know where Jimmy
was.

As Anna left Lucius' house, she talked to herself when she sat down in her car, "Well, at least I found out Jimmy went to Madison and that gives us a location with a decent opportunity to uncover clues about where he went with his family. I'm especially excited about the reference to Eva; I hope there is a pot of significant information at the end of that rainbow."

Anna unclipped her cell phone and rang up Uncle Marv. Now, Uncle Marv on the phone and Uncle Marv in person are two different people. The on-the-phone Uncle Marv is very formal and curt. "Oh, hello Anna, what is the occasion of this phone call?"

Anna told Uncle Marv about *Fifteen Decisive Battles of the World* with the comment in it about Eva.

"That sentence Jakob wrote makes no sense to me, Anna."

"Was Eva a farmer, Uncle Marv?"

"No, Anna, that's why it makes no sense. Check out Eva's deposition that you copied out of my Jakob Meyer file regarding Gertrude's claim to Jacob's Civil War pension. In that deposition, she explains her station in life. I can't remember right now what it was, but I know it wasn't a farmer."

"Thanks, Uncle Marv, that helps. How are you doing today?"

"Oh, just fine, Anna, just fine."

Anna was accustomed to Uncle Marv's telephone manner, so she said good bye and drove back to her flat to review Eva's deposition of 1905. "Uncle Marv was right. This is what Eva outlined about her life. 'I was born in Boston, the daughter of Rebecca and Jakob Meyer. At an early age, I went to live with my Great Uncle in Boston and worked in his department store until I was 14. Then I went to Augusta, Maine, to be near my mother. I also worked in a department store there until I left permanently for Minnesota, met Alexander Gant there, and married him in 1867. We lived in my father's house that had been sitting empty until it was given to me. Alexander was a lawyer and practiced law in Rockford until he died five years ago. When the last of our three children left home, I went to work in my husband's law firm and am still there today.'

"No mention of farming, so what does Jakob's message mean?" Anna was talking to herself out loud again.

Anna called Jack at his law office and explained what she had found. What happened to the lover in her? She was all business.

Jack asked a few questions and suggested they get together soon. "Let's have dinner tonight at Murray's, at our usual table, and talk strategy. Write down the exact words from the decisive battles book so we can brainstorm what they may mean. If there are any underlined words or other marks or clues on that page, make sure to note them.

"Sorry to rush, but I need to be at the Ramsey County Courthouse in 20 minutes. I do have one last message for you though."

"And what would that be, Mr. Quinn?"

"I love you, Anna, with all my heart, and the day can't go fast enough until I see you tonight."

"I love you too, Jack, my darling, and I'm looking forward to tonight as much as you are." I could see a change in her face. She had been tense when she called Jack; now she was relaxed and happy. The lover had returned.

Anna rushed back to her office to see who was available for a team meeting. It was her lucky day. They were all there and could all meet at 3:30 p.m.

"Well, guys, I talked to Lucius Gant and I honestly think he doesn't know where Jimmy is, except that he went to Madison, Wisconsin, to pick up his wife and daughter and then into hiding somewhere. Jacob Gant wouldn't talk to us and nothing turned up at Jimmy's house. Where do you suggest we go from here?

Tony was the first to talk. "Why don't a couple of us go to Madison and see what we can dig up? Maybe someone there knows where they went. I volunteer to be one, and I'd like Michael to accompany me if for no other reason than having some luck of the Irish to bolster us?"

"Oh, some Irish luck now you're asking for," responded Michael with a grin. "If it's luck you desire, I'm your man. What's your call, Anna, my dear?"

"Thanks for volunteering. I was ready to go to Madison myself, but I've the genealogy side of the case that suddenly needs some attention back here." Anna explained the two notes she had found in the book in Eldridge Gant's library, one of which raised her suspicion that the money in the tin box was tainted and the other gave her hope to discover more about Eva, if the riddle could be figured out.

"When can you two leave?"

"Would tomorrow be up to your standards?" answered Michael.

"How about the day after?" asked Tony. My son has a basketball game tomorrow night, and I don't want to miss it. He doesn't play much, but he appreciates my coming to the games, and I don't want him to feel I can miss games because he's not the star."

Anna nodded her head. "OK then, you depart on Friday. It might be good to have a weekend to talk to more people. Stay there as long as you need to."

Anna was alone at her desk after the meeting; everyone else had cleared out. She had two hours until dinner with Jack, and Murray's was just seven blocks down the street from her office, mostly by skyways. Anna was appropriately dressed for Murray's – a grey blazer, blue pants, and a white blouse – so there was no reason to change clothes at her flat. She decided to allocate the time writing a few paragraphs on a notepad to transfer to her journal at a later time. I had seen her do that before.

"Here I am a mature woman of 34, with a career of being tough with criminals, and I feel like a little schoolgirl meeting Jack tonight. He told me he loved me and can hardly wait until we meet tonight. He's bringing me into a whole new world, a world of love that I'm finding exciting.

"I talked to Gramma McGrath last night too late to record the conversation in my journal. When I told her how things were progressing with Jack, I could tell how thrilled she was. 'Anna, you won't regret marrying Jack, but you'll regret not marrying him.' I never said anything to her about marrying Jack. But once she planted the idea in my head, I have not been able to get it out. Yes, marry Jack. I think it will be some time before he asks me again. He'll want to be certain I have placed him ahead of my job. It will take time.

"If he asked me tonight if I'd marry him, I'd say yes. But I need to be patient and allow him to propose from his comfort zone. When he does pop the question, this time I'll be ready."

Ah, love, what a mixed blessing to the human species. At its best, it brings great joy to men and women; and at its worst, it causes wars to be fought and kingships to be given up. So much of human history, literature, music, and individual life revolve around love. If love did not exist, the zest for life would be greatly diminished, the world would be bleak, despair and depression would rule the world.

I'm looking forward to being with Anna and Jack for dinner tonight; there'll be an extra chair for me. What will happen to them in the weeks and months ahead? I'm glad I can't see into the future, for it would eliminate the anticipation.

CHAPTER EIGHT

RUMMAGING THROUGH THE GANT LIBRARY

Jack asked his secretary to call for a reservation at Murray's for 6:30 p.m., and Anna left work early enough to be there by 6:20. She was ushered to a table at the very back, just in front of the piano (which only was in use on Friday and Saturday nights), and the most private table in the establishment; it was their table, always their table, because Jack was a special customer, on the A-list so to speak.

Anna ordered a glass of Merlot, perhaps to calm the jittery nerves that had assailed her for the two hours after the team meeting while she had anxiously been waiting to have dinner with Jack. She had been quite a sight in her office, shuffling papers around, writing notes for her journal, preening her hair, and fine tuning what little makeup she wore. She breathed deeply, sipped the wine, and I could visibly see her relax. She seemed mentally prepared for Jack, with a look of calm anticipation, but now it was his turn to be late. Jack nearly pushed a client out the door of his office at 6:10 and was fortunate traffic was not heavy, arriving at Murray's at 6:40 and giving Anna a kiss at 6:45. "I can't admonish you for being late, given that I was the culprit last time. What happened?" Jack explained his dilemma to Anna's satisfaction.

Should I report their conversation as they ordered their steak-for-two dinner, waited for it to be delivered, and consumed it slowly? I think not. The conversation between two people in love is predictable and somewhat tiresome to anyone other than themselves. It's at the end of the dinner that I want to be an active reporter again.

With the dinner concluded, Jack asked, "Should I order two Irish coffees for us, Anna, before we plunge into some serious genealogy?"

"I think I'll pass on the coffee, Jack, if you don't mind."

"Oh, but I do mind, Anna. What's the use of being Irish if you don't have Irish coffee after a meal now and again, especially for such a momentous occasion as this?" Jack had a smile on his face that was hard to resist.

"All right, Jack," Anna said with amusement in her voice. I'll have an Irish coffee. Are you satisfied now?"

"Most assuredly I am."

Halfway through the coffee, Anna handed Jack a photocopy of the page out of *Fifteen Decisive Battles of the World* showing both a note for Elizabeth Meyer, Jakob's wife, telling her where the coins were hidden and the note about Eva.

> If you wanna know more about Eva pretend her a farmer and the
> story is on page 440.

"I've been thinking about that message all afternoon," voiced Jack, "and about Uncle Marv saying Eva was never a farmer. What do you think, Anna?"

"I believe the clues to the message are in the words pretend, farmer, and the page numbers of supposedly a book; so I pondered on those words and asked myself, 'If I were Eva and a farmer and were looking for a book, what kind of book would it be?"

"Brilliant, Anna. Your detective mind is at 100 %. She'd be looking for a book about farming."

"That's a good possibility," replied Anna. "Let's visit the Gant house tomorrow and rummage around in the books and see what we find. Can you take off a couple hours?"

"I've the morning open, Anna, but I'm booked for the afternoon. What about you?

"The morning it is, then," said Anna, with a wink of her eye to Jack, which sent shivers through his body. Oh, love, when it is on the front burner, all that happens speaks to it. That's the way it was becoming for Anna and Jack.

"There is one other matter I'd like to bounce off you, Jack. I have become more and more uncomfortable with how Jakob obtained $1,450 of newly minted gold and silver coins. Take a look at this part of the first note to Elizabeth, after telling her where to find the Civil War coins."

I tradded most of $5000 in greenbacks I depossited in 3 St. Paul
banks duren the war fer the brandy new gold and silver coins when
I were mustered out of service at Fort Snelling on April 29, 1864.

"I forgot to tell you about the discussion I had with Uncle Marv
two Saturdays ago, when you were in Chicago. It was a tough week
for him with a viral infection, his blood sugar dropping to under 80,
and Thanksgiving. His memory was lagging, and the only information
he dispensed was that Jakob was probably so poor getting started on
the farm that he enlisted in the First Minnesota for the money. I did
some research on Civil War pay and found there was a $100 bonus for
signing up at that time, and a private received only $13 a month in
greenbacks. For an enlistment of three years that wouldn't even be
$600 total. I asked if the money could have been an inheritance from
his father or someone else during the war. A direct question seemed to
improve his memory.

"Uncle Marv said he had the same thought about the money and
researched census records in Maine, and Jakob's father was still alive
when Jakob met an untimely death in his wood bin. Uncle Marv
thought that if anyone would have received an inheritance from
another relative, it would have been his father, not Jakob. We
discussed Jakob bouncing all over the place, putting his wife in an
insane asylum, and traveling a long distance to Minnesota, where he
married again, and left his new wife on her own when he joined the
army three months after their nuptials. We both felt Jakob was a bit of
a scoundrel and the money he had in three St. Paul banks may not have
been honest dollars. Why would he have put money in three banks,
after all? It's as if he were trying to hide something." Anna may have
forgotten to pass this information on to Jack, but she hadn't forgotten
the details. After one and a half weeks, it may seem unusual for
someone to remember so much of a conversation, but Anna's job was
to remember large amounts of details for long amounts of time, and
she excelled at it. It's like a doctor who can remember all the
contraindications of a drug one year after she has researched the
information.

I could see Jack was surprised by this information. "I don't mean
to be critical of you Anna, my dear, but I'm bewildered that you didn't
tell me about your discussion with Marv before. I've been so busy

with legal work that it slipped my mind that you would be talking to him about Jakob Meyer that Saturday."

"I'm bewildered also, Jack. It's not like me not to disclose critical information. I wasn't hiding anything from you; the truth is it slipped my mind too. I've been so caught up in trying to find the conspirator of the murder of Eldridge Gant, attempting to understand the genealogy that leads to the coins, and captivated with one other matter that has attacked the clarity of my thinking."

Jack innocently asked, "And what would that one other matter be, Anna?"

I knew what was coming because I had been observing it myself. Anna was not behaving like herself. She was not the focused, organized person she customarily was. There was something happening to her that had turned her life upside down – she was in love. She reached across the dinner table and put her hand on Jack's.

"I'm in love with you, Jack, my darling, and it's as if I'm walking in a fog. My job is no longer first in my mind, not the murder or the genealogy; you are, and it is a wonderful and terrible thing at the same time. I am the happiest I've been my whole life, but I'm so distracted I'm afraid I'm going to come to work some day in my nightgown. The matter of where Jakob obtained the money became dissipated in the cloud. I'm sorry."

Jack was speechless for several moments, and held Anna's hand tightly, as tears were rolling down his cheeks. When he finally composed himself he spoke softly, "You have overwhelmed me. I didn't know you were in the same straits I have been in since we got back together. My co-workers think I've been moonstruck, and they are right. I forget to do the simplest things. In court yesterday, a client had to ask me if I were going to object to what the prosecuting attorney had just asked a witness. I too was in a fog, and it was so embarrassing."

"What are we going to do, Jack? We can't go on like this or we'll be out on the street looking for new jobs."

"I could ask you to marry me right now, Anna, my love, but I think we need to work through the walking-in-a-fog dawning of love and onto firm ground so we both make a decision based on a deeper commitment to live the rest of our days together. It's hard for me to say that because I would love to marry you tomorrow."

Jack was being the practical person he was, but it was a smart decision. I have seen people caught up in the moonstruck side of love, marry, and divorce in a year when the glitter wears off. True love accepts that one's partner may not always screw the toothpaste cap back on.

Anna responded, "My emotions have control of me right now, but as I slip into my mind, I realize the logic of what you are saying."

They sat holding hands for more than a minute without saying anything more. Anna broke the silence. "What do you think, Jack, about the money? I may not be the heir to any of it or may be the heir to half of it or all of it. I know I'd want no part of the money if it's questionable."

"I'd say you shouldn't refuse any part of the money that comes to you; it would go back to the government. Give it away to a worthy cause, like a disabled veterans' charity. Wherever Jakob found the money, it was during the war, and it would be most fair that it should go back to soldiers." Even if Anna and Jack had known that Jakob had stolen the money from dead soldiers, as I do, they couldn't have made a better choice of how to dispose of it, if needed.

It was the 65th anniversary of Pearl Harbor the next day, as Jack's car pulled into the driveway of Eldridge Gant's house in Rockford, and he quickly circumvented the car to open Anna's door for her, not that she wasn't fully capable of opening her own door, but Jack was a gentleman and who better to be a gentleman to than his one true love. Anna was pleased with this show of affection.

Now, why would I mention the anniversary of Pearl Harbor? I have a great distaste for wars because many young people lose the years allotted to them, and World War II adjusted the natural time of death for 72 million men, women, and children. Estimates of deaths ranged from 50-70 million, but I was there, and I know the right number.

The house was still yellow taped. Anna led the way to the summer kitchen door, through the house, and up the stairs to the sky parlor room, aka the library. "Well, there are a good number of books here," stated Jack, "and I see there is a small bookcase out in the hallway also. I suggest you start with the horizontal bookcase on the south wall, I'll start with the bookcase in the hallway, and we'll work our way to the large bookcase on the southwest wall."

"This is exciting," remarked Anna, and bestowed a kiss on Jack's lips before they separated to opposite starting points.

After ten minutes, they were both at the large bookcase, having found nothing so far. Jack took the top shelves and Anna the bottom ones. A few minutes later Jack was startled by a loud cry, "What about this, Jack? I've found a likely book – *The Gentleman Farmer*." The book she had just found was written by Lord Henry Kames in 1776.

They stood together as Anna hurriedly paged to the end of the book. The last page of the book was 438, with a large "Finis" written on it. "The book ends two pages short of 440," said Anna with exasperation in her voice."

"But there are blank pages after that," said Jack. "The first blank page facing the last page of the book would be 439. If we turn that page over..." A gasp escaped from both of them simultaneously. There was a note on that page written by Jakob Meyer.

> Lizabeth-
> I kno youll find this note cause youre smart. I didna want no one else to find it and tear it up. Its not importint to you cause youre my wife but its importint to our child you are carrying cause Daniels sickly and wont live much longer. You know bout Eva, the child of my frist marriage but I nevir told you she was no child of mine and I don't want her to have nothen of mine but you get it all and our child. My first wife Rebecca was pregnant 4 months comen into our marriage but she nevir tole me. At 6 months she couldn't hide it any more. I forced her to tell the father. it was a person named Charles Gravely. It broke our marriage apart and aftir 3 years Becca went insane and I committed her to the asylum in Maine.
> your husband Jakob

There was more than a minute of silence as Anna and Jack read over the note several times. Jack was the first to speak. "The information in this note is astonishing, Anna. It is a major genealogical breakthrough for us. Jakob has confirmed that Eva was illegitimate *and* that he was the father of Gertrude. The only thing missing is whether Jakob divorced his first wife, but I'd conjecture he had because he would be smart enough to know his second marriage was not valid if he had not divorced Rebecca and there would be no inheritance for either Elizabeth or Gertrude. We've hit a gold mine."

"You're wearing your genealogical hat, Jack, and your excitement stems from that. I'm very excited also about this message. But we both need to put on our legal hats. This is information to fill out a genealogical chart, but it is not information that would hold up in a probate court, and that's where this case will end up. We need to find legal records that substantiate what Jakob has told us, but his information will help guide what legal information we look for."

"You're absolutely right, Anna. I've been in enough probate courts to know we need legal information. It's time for me to go to Boston for a week, but that won't be possible until January. I have a number of cases that need resolving before the end of the year. I'll block out the second week of January, if that's all right with you."

"We can work around your schedule, Jack, and I need to concentrate on finding Jimmy Gant anyway."

This time it was Jack's turn to show affection. He embraced Anna in a way that only lovers embrace. "We make a great team, Anna, and I'm not saying that just about the genealogy search we are on. I love everything about you, and I'm starting to come out of the fog I've been walking in and onto more solid ground. One of these days I may just drop to my knees and ask you to marry me, so be ready."

"I'll be ready. I'm coming out of the fog also."

Jack took Anna back to her office in the Grain Exchange building and headed back to St. Paul for a 2 p.m. court appearance.

That evening I watched Anna write in her journal.

"There was something magical about my seeing my great-great-grandfather's handwriting again, especially now it appears he really is my ancestor, even though Uncle Marv was probably right about his being a scoundrel.

"I've come to the conclusion that I won't accept any part of the proceeds of the coins in the tin box; I will give it away if any of it is mine and will tell that both to my team and to my supervisor. The legal part of this and the personal part are what motivate me now. The disposition of the coins is tied up with Eldridge Gant, and I want to wrap up all the loose ends in his murder. On the personal side, I have no desire to obtain any money from this, but I am fascinated by the mystery of what my lineage is back to the end of the Civil War and the mysteries that surround my ancestors.

"When I talked to Gramma McGrath about being in love with Jack and that we'll probably be married one day, she was in seventh heaven. Knowing her, I'll bet she's been praying for this for a long time. 'An Irish girl shouldn't be single,' were her words to me a few months back.

"I have a feeling something interesting is going to happen at work Monday. I wonder what it will be."

CHAPTER NINE

MACK FREIGHTER COPS A PLEA

The morning of December 10 arose with a sunny sky, a five degree temperature, and a brisk wind, a typical winter day in Minneapolis. Anna stared out her front balcony window, and announced to herself, "Ah, there is nothing like bright sunshine to start the week. All weekend I've sensed a surprise lying in wait for me at work today, wondering when it will jump up and grab me." Two characteristics that establish Anna as an outstanding detective are her intuition and her discernment, gifts she was born with.

Anna pulled out of her Heritage Landing parking lot, drove down 1st Street to 3rd Avenue, took a left at 4th Street and was at the Grain Exchange building. Traffic was light, allowing her to reach her office in less than fifteen minutes. As she stepped out of the elevator on the sixth floor at 8:00 a.m. sharp, she encountered Sylvia Johnson who had been furiously pacing back and forth in the hallway, like a Union messenger waiting to tell his commanding officer he had just discovered the location of General Lee. Sylvia was almost breathless when she ran up to Anna. "You're not going to believe what happened five minutes ago."

"You've found Jimmy Gant?"

"Not quite that dramatic, Anna, but dramatic. One of the thugs who killed Eldridge Gant wants to talk to us without Jacob Gant, his lawyer."

"Which one?" asked Anna, who was now as excited as Sylvia.

"Mack Freighter," replied Sylvia, still trying to catch her breath. "He was the quiet one of the two when I interrogated them; the talkative one was Toby Levias."

"Where is Mack now, Sylvia?" asked Anna who herself was fighting hyperventilation.

"In the interrogation room inside, waiting for you. We all felt you should question him, since you have a knack of obtaining the most information from a criminal."

"Sylvia, I just knew something special was about to happen today. Now I know what it is."

The interrogation room measured 10 feet by 12 feet and was filled with video and audio recording equipment; it was not designed to make the person being questioned comfortable. Anna rocked back in one of the two office chairs in the room and adopted a more casual questioning technique. Mack was in the second chair around the corner of a wall desk and seemed relieved with the relaxed atmosphere created by Anna.

"I'm Anna Fitzgerald, the lead detective on this case, Mack. We appreciate your coming here to talk to us. Have you been treated well in jail these last two months?"

"The guards are decent, but it seems more like five months than two. I've been doin a lot of thinkin lately."

"What have you been thinking about, Mack?" Anna was actually smiling during an interrogation. I had never seen that before.

"I've been thinkin I'm facin life in prison. Is that right, detective?"

"That's right, Mack." The smile left Anna's face.

"Would it be less if I tole you Toby was the one who did all the torturin and killin and I just stood by?"

"That would make you an accomplice, and by law an accomplice has the same degree of guilt as the person he or she is assisting and faces the same criminal penalties. If you two had murdered Eldridge and escaped free, then perhaps a lesser term could be negotiated for you if you came forward to finger Toby. But you were both caught in the act, and there is nothing you have to offer to cop a plea."

Mack had a look on his face as if he had received the worst news of his life, which in fact he had.

"I guess I'm shit out of luck," said Mack with a tremor in his voice.

"Maybe not, Mack," said Anna quickly, "I suspect you and Toby were hired by Jimmy Gant to commit this murder. If you can tell me about that and where Jimmy is, I would be willing to go to the District Attorney's office to plea bargain on your behalf. I can't promise you anything, other than I would go to bat for you."

"If I give you that information, Jimmy would have me killed."

"Not if he doesn't know where you are. We have ways of protecting you." Anna was leaning forward in her chair, and her approach became persuasive and direct. "You came to see me to receive a lesser sentence. It would be a risk on your part, but we wouldn't hang you out to dry. You'd have to trust us. There are no guarantees, but your odds of coming out of this alive are quite good."

Mack sat in his chair with his head down for two minutes without saying anything. Anna did not press him. I could almost hear the gears whirring in his head, and then he looked up. "I'll take the chance to avoid life in prison. Here's what happened. All communication was tween Jimmy and Toby, so I don't know all the details. Jimmy asked Toby if we was willin to drag information out of Eldridge Gant as to where a tin box was hidden in his house. That was the end of September somewhere. Jimmy told Toby he'd give us $5,000 the day before we went to Eldridge's house in Rockford and another $5,000 when we gived him the tin box.

"Then on October 10, Jimmy left a message for Toby to say he needed to leave town right away because his life was in danger, and he'd get back to us when he returned."

"How do you know the exact date, Mack?"

"It was the day my ex-wife fetched me to court cause I hadn't paid her money from the divorce agreement."

"I see; continue with your story," said Anna. She was leaning back in her chair again with a relaxed look on her face, I suspect because she didn't feel the need to pressure him as long as he was supplying information freely.

"Well, Jimmy called again and gave Toby his father's phone number, and then Toby called the father – I think his name is Lucius – and he gave Toby $5,000 he said was from Jimmy. Toby thanked him and thought that was the end of it. But Jimmy's father said no, he was in communication with Jimmy, and his son wanted us to go through with forcin Eldridge to tell us where the tin box was hidden and then kill him, and we'd git another $5,000 when the job was done and

Lucius had the tin box to give to Jimmy. He said he was actin as an agent for Jimmy who was in hidin. We went to the house the next day, and you know the rest."

I noticed Anna was astonished by this information but confused by the sequence of Toby's story; there were pieces missing. She had made a mistake in believing she had extracted all the information that Lucius knew. I wish I could have told her that at the time; I thought she'd perhaps never find out the true story because of her misguided trust in Lucius. I've found over the centuries that when truth is cloaked in one instance, it comes back later in a different set of clothes. I was as surprised as Anna that Mack would be truth in prison clothes. Ten seconds passed slowly until Anna was able to regain her composure.

"This will help immensely, Mack, but to plea bargain with the District Attorney's office, I need one more critical piece of intelligence from you. Where did Jimmy go? Our goal is to arrest him and interrogate him before we bring this case to trial, so we have the full picture of what happened; and the better information you give us, the better will be the odds of your receiving a reduced sentence. Do you understand that?"

"I understan, but remember I aint got all the details Toby has, and I don't think he'll be willin to talk to you."

"Just tell me what you know, Mack, and be complete and put it in the right order."

"OK. Jimmy left a phone message for Toby that somethin bad happened with his drug business, and he had to pick up his wife and daughter in Madison and all go hide in New York. Toby called Jimmy back and said to him that a deal had been agreed to and it didn look like it would pull off, and we should git some money for our trouble. Jimmy said he had to think bout it, and then Jimmy called back soon and gave Toby his father's phone number an I told you all bout that."

Anna looked pleased with the knowledge that Jimmy was in New York, but she went a step further with Mack. "Do you know where in New York he went, Mack? If you do, it will strengthen your case for a reduced sentence." Anna was acting as if Mack were her best friend, and her focus was in helping him.

"Toby asked him where in New York, Jimmy tole him, and Toby tole me: but I don't remember. I never been to New York."

"Was it Brooklyn?"

"No."

"How about Queens or Harlem?"

"I don't think so."

"Does Manhattan sound familiar?"

"Yes, that's it. Jimmy tole Toby he had a high school friend living in…is there a Lower Manhattan?"

"Yes there is."

"Then that's what he said –Lower Manhattan."

Now why, you may ask, was Jimmy so open with Toby about his whereabouts? Through their time together laying out the plans for obtaining the tin box, Jimmy and Toby bonded, kind of like the spirit of death and the spirit of violence would bond. It's always been interesting to me how evil people can bond so much more quickly and securely than most people not so villainous, who bond more closely with themselves than anyone else. Yet such openness was a grave mistake on Jimmy's part. Toby, true to his part of the bond, would never tell anyone about Jimmy's whereabouts; however Toby and Mack were heavy drinkers, and one night that information just slipped out of Toby's mouth as he and Mack were hoisting beer after beer after beer. Drinking is the great liberator of information.

It must have been difficult for Anna to stay calm with the facts Mack had just revealed, but I expect she didn't want Mack to observe how excited she was. "Thank you very much for cooperating with me, Mack. If the information you have given me helps us arrest Jimmy Gant, I will go to bat for you with the District Attorney's office. In the meantime, don't talk to anyone about our meeting."

"You can count on that!" said Mack.

Anna sat in the interrogation room after Mack headed back to his jail cell across the street, heavily guarded, and had a discussion with herself. "That was amazing; I never expected to receive such critical information from Mack, a virtual roadmap to find Jimmy Gant. It's time for a team meeting."

Before Anna could deliver a message for a meeting that day, her supervising lieutenant called her into his office. She was the assigned day case person, meaning all incoming cases were assigned to her that particular day. Dispatch had just reported a shooting in a bar in

Medina, with four people killed. "You need to head out there right now, Anna, to investigate. Three people in the bar who were not shot need to be questioned."

Anna replied, "Seven people in a bar on a Monday morning? How pathetic. And what has happened to the shooter, Lieutenant?"

"He ran out the door and is long gone. We don't even know what car he was driving. There are two Medina officers on the scene who can fill you in on the details."

The team meeting would have to wait a few days.

By Friday, December 14, the Medina shooter had been apprehended and space reappeared in Anna's schedule. It was 9:30 a.m. and the team was on the front burner to receive the hot news Anna had referred to in a brief e-mail she had sent them late Monday evening. When she explained what Mack had revealed to her, they were bubbling with excitement.

Joe Wilshire said what everyone knew. "This should be easy. We find out where Jimmy went to high school and run backgrounds on everyone who was in his class and who would now be living in Lower Manhattan. I'd be surprised if there were more than one."

"At my last two class reunions," said Sylvia, "there were two people that no one could locate; it's as if they disappeared off the face of the earth. I hope that isn't the case here, but I'm throwing in that caveat."

"What Sylvia said could happen," commented Michael, "but I'll volunteer to do the research to mix in the luck of the Irish."

Anna shook her head and laughed at Michael's comment. "Will that be the same luck of the Irish as when you went to the wrong house for a domestic dispute in Rockford and made the front page of the Wright County Journal-Press?"

Michael smiled. "Oh, Anna, you can be so cruel that it breaks my heart. Would that be anything like the time you made a domestic abuse call and arrested the husband who was being beaten by his wife?"

"I will throw no more stones, Michael," returned Anna, throwing her arms up in the air in surrender. "We all have too many skeletons in our closet. All right, Michael, you do the research. I'd suggest you start with the senior year and, if needed, go back to the junior year for anyone not in the senior yearbook and so forth to the sophomore year if necessary."

"I will follow your directions scrupulously, Anna, my darling, and we will find our man. I guarantee it."

"I'd like to discuss another item with all of you," ventured Anna. "My master genealogist boyfriend Jack is heading to Boston the second week of January to research the parentage of Eva Meyer and find if there is any legal evidence of the divorce of Jakob Meyer, my probable great-great-grandfather, and his first wife. The results of that search could show I am a partial heir to the Civil War coins, no heir at all, or the only heir. However, I want to declare to you now that I have found enough evidence to put a dark cloud around that money and have no intention of receiving any part of it, no matter what happens. I'll donate whatever belongs to me to a charity for disabled veterans. That should eliminate any conflict of interest."

"I think you're right, Anna," said Tony Talridge. "However, I'd run that by our lieutenant for his take."

"Thanks, Tony, I'll do that right now, since I think we've covered everything here.

"To what do I owe this surprise?" asked Lieutenant Daily with a smile on his face. Anna was his favorite detective because she was always cheerful, optimistic, and efficiently solved all the crimes he assigned to her.

"I want to discuss with you the genealogy side of the Eldridge Gant murder, the conclusion of which will resolve who the Civil War coins belong to."

Lieutenant Daily viewed Anna with a professional gaze. "Do you know whether you are an heir or not?"

Anna briefed him on what she had found out thus far genealogically concerning her possible claim to the coins and the team meeting she just walked away from. "If I declare that, even if I'm an heir, I'll give the coins away to a charity, will that absolve me from any conflict of interest?"

"I trust you'll do what you have just declared, and that eliminates you from personal gain if any or all of the coins belong to you, but we need to make your declaration legal and binding for the sake of transparency. I'll call our lawyer at the Hennepin County Government Center, give him the background, and then you can walk over there and meet with him. He'll draw up a document that you'll sign and I'll sign and that will end any accusations of conflict of interest."

And so that's what Anna did that same day.

Michael O'Hara's grand plans to discover the friend of Jimmy's in the Washburn yearbooks of 1990, 1991, and 1992 ran into a delay when Michael was assigned four hot cases as the day case person the Monday after the team meeting, and was inundated with investigations during the next two weeks. The Christmas season should be a season of love and peace, but it's often a time of hatred and crime, mainly thefts and domestics. This year was no different. The other team members also had their turns as the day case person and racked up more work to triage with the Eldridge Gant case.

Michael finally tackled the yearbooks the first week of January. Anna volunteered to help Michael in the yearbook search, and Joe, Tony, and Sylvia volunteered to conduct the necessary background searches. They were on a fast track with the nearly three-week delay.

It would be a laborious process, especially if they were required to dig into the 1990 yearbook. But Anna, always looking how to be more efficient, had a plan to speed up the process. "Michael, let's talk to administrators and teachers who were here during those years and ask if they remember Jimmy Gant and who might have been good friends of his. Then we can find those friends in the yearbook and have the rest of the team do backgrounds on them."

That turned out to be a wonderful idea. There are two kinds of people remembered during their high school years – those who are very popular and do momentous things and those who are known as hard cases and do terrible things. The students at Columbine after nearly eight years have perhaps forgotten many of their classmates, but I doubt that any of them has forgotten the names of the two teenagers who gunned down their classmates.

Jimmy fit into the latter category, and the principal of the school when Jimmy attended Washburn was yet the principal and remembered Jimmy from many hours spent with him in his office.

Three others associated with Jimmy fit into the same category, and the principal remembered their names as well – Jared Aldrich, Paul Boswell, and Jim Peachie.

Michael called the names back to Tony and within two days the backgrounds were completed and one Paul Boswell was shown as living in lower Manhattan, in a condo and townhome development on Wall Street. Tony called the development and found that Jimmy's friend was still living there.

Anna enlisted herself to go to New York and requested that the veteran Tony Talridge accompany her. Michael pleaded, "Anna, my dear, won't you be taking me also? I grew up in New York City and may be of logistical help."

"Michael, are you sure you don't just want to go with us so you can visit the Irish cronies you left behind?"

"Well, that could be an incentive, but the arresting of Jimmy Gant comes first."

The imploring look on Michael's face made Anna crack up. "You're an incurable Irishman, Michael. You think you can get anything you fancy. All right, we'll go as three instead of two. Your knowledge of New York may in fact be an asset. But that's the only reason you're going. And yes, you can see your Irish friends if there is an opportunity."

Michael smiled his impish smile and said gleefully. "Oh, thank you, Anna. I will not disappoint you. We'll get our man."

It ended up that Jack would be in Boston at the same time Anna, Tony, and Michael would be in New York, just two hundred miles away – Jack working on the genealogy and the other three fixed on finding Jimmy Gant.

That night Anna wrote in her journal: "Jack was thrilled when I told him I'd be only 200 miles from him next week, but we agreed we'd probably both be too busy to arrange a rendezvous. Yet, I feel better having him closer than Minneapolis.

"Jack asked if we could be together the whole weekend. 'I need to immerse myself in you, Anna, to bolster me for not seeing you the following week.' Oh, how I love him! I need bolstering this weekend also to get me through the next week. I don't really want to do anything special Saturday and Sunday; I just want to hang around him. That last sentence sounds like we're married already – not a date but just hanging around.

"So, pleasure this weekend and hard work next week."

CHAPTER TEN

JACK QUINN IN BOSTON

Jack landed at Logan Airport in Boston early Sunday afternoon, rented a car at the airport, and drove four miles to his hotel on Beacon Street. When he entered his room, the first thing he did was call Anna.

"I'm here safe and sound Anna, and ready to start in tomorrow morning at a government building that houses vital records. I wanted to call you before you took off to tell you I love you more and more each day, and I'll miss you tremendously."

"And I love you, Jack, with all my heart. We're at the airport now and will be boarding in less than a half hour. How's your hotel?

"Spectacular; it would be perfect if you were here. I'm looking at an ornate fireplace right now in my room, a huge mahogany desk that will serve me well in compiling notes, and all else expansive and well appointed. Their on-line site understated the luxury of the hotel."

"I'm happy you have a nice place, Jack. I'm afraid our rooms won't match up to yours – government budget, you know." There was a pause in their conversation. "Jack, they're boarding our flight early. I have to go now. Stay in touch as you find out things. I love you."

"Have a good flight, Anna. I love you too."

Jack had tears in his eyes when he put down the phone. He went over to the desk, pulled a sheet of paper off a pad, and wrote a poem to Anna.

> You are the sun, moon, and stars above,
> and the earth beneath my feet.
> My thoughts are consumed with you by day,
> and you visit me in my dreams at night.

This poem is not a literary masterpiece, but I thought I'd include it to give a glimpse into Jack's feelings for Anna.

The following morning the weather was beautiful for January 8 in Boston – clear skies, no wind, and 44 degrees – so Jack decided to take the subway to the Massachusetts Registry of Vital Records and Statistics down in Dorchester. It took him six minutes to walk from his hotel to the Downtown Crossing, where he took the Red Line subway to the JFK/UMass exit, and walked another six minutes to the Registry, next to the Bayside Expo Center. Monday's mission was to find the legal date Eva was born. Jack had done a cursory investigation of where to visit in Boston in the weeks before he left; he was too busy to do a full search, but he should have carved out more time to understand the Commonwealth of Massachusetts in general and Boston specifically.

When he reached the information desk, he was confronted with his lack of due diligence in researching the on-line information available. Back in Minneapolis, he had found the phone number of the Registry and called; however, the person he had talked to had given him the wrong information. Today he received the correct information. "I'm sorry sir, but this site only maintains birth certificates from 1921 to the present."

Jack slumped down with his elbows on the desk, which was about stomach high for him, and feigned to pull out his hair. "Is that information on-line?" Jack asked the man behind the desk.

"Yes it's right on the home page. Did you check our web site?"

"No, but I should have," said Jack with a frustrated look, "and then I wouldn't be standing here in the wrong place. Now I suppose you're about to tell me I need to go back to downtown Boston to find birth certificates from the 1850s." He was laughing, but it was a laugh of irony, not humor: here was the successful trial lawyer who depended on thorough research, and he couldn't even find the right location to do his genealogical research in Boston.

The man behind the desk also laughed, but this was a friendly laugh. "You're in luck. You don't have to go back to Boston. The Massachusetts Archives is only three miles south of here, and that's where you'll find what you're looking for."

Jack thanked him kindly and went outside to hail a cab; it was too far to walk.

Jack walked through the front door of the Massachusetts Archives and headed to the information desk, where the receptionist confirmed that births, marriages, and deaths could be found here from 1841 to 1920.

"I called last week and inquired if divorces could be accessed here. I was told they were available from 1785 to 1887. Is that true?" Jack had a look on his face and a posture in his body that seemed to be saying, "I probably have the wrong information again."

"Yes, that's true; however, it's not a simple process. Divorces during those years went through Judicial Courts, so you'll need to look through the Judicial Archives, and you'll need to know the judicial district in which the divorce was recorded."

"Is there someone who can help me with that?" Jack asked politely.

"Oh, yes, but you'll have to come back tomorrow morning for that. The most knowledgeable person in the Judicial Archives, Lawrence Tippet, is not here this afternoon."

To Jack, the words "you'll have to" were irritating. I remember one time in a clothing store where Jack had just bought a very expensive suit and was told, "You'll have to come back tomorrow to be fitted." Jack's response to that clerk was framed in a tone of mild anger and sarcastic curtness, "No, I don't have to come back tomorrow to be fitted. You can keep your suit, and I'll go to your competitor at the other end of the mall and buy a suit from them, and be fitted today. I don't have time to come back tomorrow."

Jack chose not to be irritated by "you'll have to" from this woman. She had a humble look and was obviously trying to be helpful. There was also a sadness in her visage that tempered Jack's reply. "Yes, I can return tomorrow morning. It's just as well. I can spend today finding the birth certificate I need. Is there someone here *now* who can help me with that?" The only sign of irritation was the mild emphasis on the word "now."

"Here she is right behind me. Jessica, could you help this person find a birth certificate?"

"It's a perfect time for me to do so," said Jessica. "And your name is…"

"Jack Quinn," he said in a tone of voice that was relieved the day was not turning out so bad after all.

"Where should we start, Jack Quinn?"

"I really need to find a marriage certificate first. Sometime in 1850, Jakob Meyer married Rebecca Jane Griffin in Boston."

Jessica responded with a smile, "You're making it too easy for me with the year and city. Usually genealogists searching out a marriage don't know the year or the place; then, we proceed painstakingly year by year and city by city, but at least there are alphabetical indexes that make the process time consuming but possible."

"My girlfriend's uncle is a genealogist, and he's done much of the groundwork for us."

Jessica knew the ropes and brought Jack to a room filled with vital records books from the various municipalities of Massachusetts, explaining to him that municipal clerks submitted registration pages to the commonwealth annually, covering the vital records generated by their offices. She picked up an index book for Boston that contained the year 1850, with the names listed alphabetically, but found no record of a marriage between Jakob Meyer and Rebecca Jane Griffin. "Are you sure of the names and the city and the year?"

"I've found that information from Uncle Marv is occasionally incomplete, like the exact date of the marriage, but I've not found any information he's given me to be inaccurate. Is it possible that a particular record wasn't indexed?"

"That's possible," answered Jessica.

"I assume the actual record books are here," stated Jack. "Could we page through the one for 1850 page by page, starting from the back?"

"Why the back?"

"Because my hypothesis is that Jakob and Rebecca were married near the end of the year and a child was born to them at the beginning of the next year."

"That will take time. Do you mind if we have lunch first?"

"Why don't you bring the book to me, Jessica, and I'll start looking through it. I'm hungrier for information right now than food."

"I'm afraid I can't let you page through the book; it would be too much wear and tear on a historical document." Jack should have known that, but his determination led him to suggest even what he knew not to be practicable.

"So what do we do then, Jessica?"

"We have microfilm you can scan, which probably will be better for you because sometimes there are added entries and corrections to what's in the record books. I'll set up 1850 for you before I go to lunch."

Given that each year contained births, marriages, and deaths, it would not be an easy task. Jack started with December and turned back day by day from the 31st. He was half-way through December when Jessica returned from lunch. "Do you need any help from me, Jack?"

"No, I've done this before, so I'll just keep plodding through. I'll let you know when I find something."

One hour later he had completed December and was starting with November. Less than halfway through, his diligence was rewarded. There was the marriage certificate for Jakob Meyer of Biddeford, Maine, age 23, to Rebecca Jane Griffin of Portland, Maine, age 16, dated November 23, 1850. This was a thrilling moment for a genealogist. I've seen people dance in circles with their hands to their heads when they find something difficult or unlikely to find. Jack didn't dance in circles, but he was having a hard time catching his breath and practically ran to find Jessica. "I've found the marriage certificate," he said breathlessly. "Can you show me where I can make a copy of it?"

"I can," said Jessica, but took care of the matter for him.

"Now let's look for the birth certificate of Eva Meyer in 1851," said Jack with more enthusiasm than he had just an hour ago. This time things went much easier. The index listed Eva Meyer as a birth and with a date. Jessica turned to the page and found a birth certificate dated April 14, 1851, showing Rebecca Jane Griffin as the mother and Jakob Meyer as the father.

"Jessica, I have a note from Jakob written in 1865 stating that he was not Eva's father but a person named Charles Gravely was. These two dates would corroborate the note that Eva was not Jakob's daughter."

"Well, Jack, even if Eva were illegitimate, she would still be listed as the daughter of the father on record when she was born. If you're looking for legal proof that Eva was not Jakob's daughter, this birth certificate will not serve the purpose. Should I make a copy of it for you anyway?"

"Yes," replied Jack dejectedly; he realized what Jessica said was true as soon as she said it, and realized it was a big brick wall in the search. "That's enough for today. I'll come back tomorrow morning and meet with Lawrence Tippet to see if we can find a divorce between Jakob and Rebecca."

"I can see you're disappointed, Jack, but maybe you'll have better luck tomorrow. If there is a divorce, it won't just be a certificate. There will be court records associated with it that spell out the reason for the divorce. At that time in this commonwealth, there weren't many acceptable reasons for divorce. Adultery is one category that comes to mind. But there are others."

Jack called Anna that evening and filled her in on what had happened in his searches that day, and she acquainted him with the progress her team had made in locating Jimmy Gant. Both of them were very tired.

"Jack, my darling, I hope we find Jimmy quickly so I can be back in Minneapolis before the end of the week, and I hope you can obtain the information you need before the end of the week. I miss you."

"I miss you too, Anna. I don't like being apart from you. I hope you are right about each of us finishing before the week is up."

They talked for another ten minutes before hanging up.

"I love you, Jack. Good night."

"I love you too Anna. Get a good night's sleep."

Tuesday morning was still warm for January, but rain was forecast for all day. Jack drove his car down to Columbia Point to spend the day at the Massachusetts Archives. He ate a huge breakfast so he wouldn't need to break for lunch.

"Is Lawrence Tippet available?" asked Jack with a smile on his face, addressing the person behind the information desk.

"I'm afraid he isn't," answered the receptionist, struggling to smile back. "He called in sick for the rest of the week. Is there anyone else who can help you?"

Yesterday had been a hard day for Jack. With this announcement, his frustration caused him to look blankly at the woman behind the desk.

"Yesterday was my first day here. Would Jessica be a knowledgeable replacement for Mr. Tippet?"

"No. Her area of expertise is births, deaths, and marriages. You must be looking for divorces if Lawrence Tippet was recommended to you.

"That's correct. I'm trying to find a divorce that may or may not have happened sometime in the 1850s," said Jack.

"In that case, you'll need to visit the Judicial Archives, which are in a separate area from where you were yesterday. Take an elevator to the second floor, and when you exit, you'll see a sign to your right that says, 'Judicial Records.' Ask for Asha Bhaskor. I personally think she is better at problem solving than Lawrence, if you are going to have problems in researching."

"Oh, I'll have problems all right. I don't know the year of the divorce, and I don't know which court it was adjudicated in."

"In that case, Asha will be just the researcher for you. She thrives on tough cases. You couldn't do better."

"Thank you so much."

"I'm glad I was able to help."

Jack walked into the Judicial Archives room and asked for Asha Bhaskor. She was a striking Indian woman who was both personable and confident. They talked in general about how to find divorces in the collection of court records. Then Asha asked, "If the divorce you are looking for was adjudicated in the city of Boston, that would be Suffolk County. If it were Middlesex County, which comprises Cambridge and Lowell, it would be easier to find."

"I think we should start with Suffolk County," ventured Jack. "The next question you'll be asking me is the year of the divorce? I think it would be in the 1850s someplace, starting with the year 1851."

"We're looking at what could turn out to be a very exhausting search, but it's just the challenge I like. I'll help you as much as I can until we find the divorce, if there is one, although it may take a week or two. From what you told me, there's no guarantee there ever was a divorce, but I know it is critical to your legal genealogy to determine if there were one. I have a suggestion so we are both busy but not doing the same thing. In the 1850s, an intent to divorce had to be published in a qualified newspaper three consecutive weeks prior to the divorce proceedings. The most likely newspaper for that would have been *The Boston Courier Weekly* because it was a qualified newspaper at the time, and had a lower advertising rate than the dailies. For genealogical work I've done, I've found it to be the best newspaper to find divorce announcements. We have that paper on microfilm covering the years 1824-1866. *The Boston Daily Advertiser*, covering the years 1836-1921 would be a good second choice. We also have that on microfilm. I'd suggest you go through both newspapers, starting with 1851."

I could see Jack was impressed by her off-hand knowledge. I would have picked Asha over Lawrence in a second. Her mind is like a steel trap; once information goes in, it never leaves. Asha set him up with the two newspapers' microfilm on separate machines, as she walked with an efficiency of movement to pour through the judicial archives of Suffolk County, starting in the year 1851 – as often as she had time to search.

And so started the laborious task of searching for the divorce of Jakob Meyer and Rebecca Jane Griffin. I must say I was intrigued to watch them in their quest – because they were on the right track, and it was only a matter of time, albeit more time probably than they anticipated, before they would be rewarded. I knew what was in the record books and what was in the microfilm of those two newspapers. Eventually there would be a jubilation that a genealogist experiences when he or she makes a "find" after much hard work.

Eight hours of searching on Tuesday, and no results. Jack called Anna that evening as usual. Wednesday was more of the same. I could see Jack becoming discouraged; I could see Asha becoming less determined. Jack called Anna that evening, and she was back in Minneapolis. Her trip had been a success, but she chose not to tell Jack about it, I would guess because she could tell in his voice that he was disheartened and she wanted to keep the focus on him. Plus he didn't ask; he was dreadfully low. "You'll find it, Jack. I know you'll find it. Keep your spirits up. I wish I could be there to help."

"I wish you were here with me right now, Anna. I need a hug and a kiss and the feel of your warm body. God, how I miss you."

Thursday dragged on with more research and no results. Jack called Anna that evening for more encouragement. Just to hear her voice seemed to bolster him.

By Friday morning, Asha was only in 1852 and Jack was just starting March 1854 in *The Boston Courier Weekly*. I was holding my breath waiting for the jolt Jack was soon to receive. He was turning through the divorce announcements in March when suddenly he jumped up in the air and screamed, "Asha, Asha, come here quickly. I found it, I found it." Asha literally ran over to the microfilm area, which was quite a sight in her floor-length skirt that she wore instead of a sari, after many years of living in the United States. "Sit down and read this, Asha," said Jack with unbounded enthusiasm. There it was, an announcement placed by Jakob Meyer stating that he would be going to court on March 22, 1854, to divorce Rebecca Jane Griffin for valid reasons. Asha was so excited she cranked to the next edition and there it was again, the same wording. And there it was again in the next edition.

Asha ran back to the judicial records area, with Jack right on her heels. She pulled out the 1854 judicial records for Suffolk County. It took her five minutes to find the court proceedings of the divorce. The trial started and ended the same day, March 22. What Jack saw in the official court recording of the divorce was more than remarkable. It was a breakthrough that was like the Union Army winning the battle of Gettysburg.

The only two witness in the court proceeding were Rebecca and Jakob. On the witness stand, Rebecca admitted she had an affair with Charles Gravely and was carrying his baby when she married Jakob. Furthermore, she admitted Charles Gravely had returned to Boston in 1853, sought the now Mrs. Meyer, and the affair recommenced. On the stand, Jakob stated he discovered the deceit in February 1854, found Charles Gravely and gave him a sound thrashing, and started proceedings to divorce Rebecca for adultery. With no other witnesses, the judge granted the divorce.

Out of fairness, I must interrupt here to present Rebecca's side of the story. I told you earlier that Jakob forced Rebecca to tell him about the affair with Charles Gravely, but I didn't tell you why he suspected an affair. Rebecca was four months pregnant when she married Jakob, but she didn't tell him. She had seen his anger and was afraid of him; she had told him before they were married that she would not be able to have intercourse with him for six months because of a feminine problem, which was not the truth, but what could she do?

By the time she was six months pregnant, she could no longer conceal her condition, and Jakob threatened to kill the child within her if she didn't tell him who the father was. She told him, but Charles Gravely was nowhere to be found. Eva was born three months later in April of 1851. I have already told you that Jakob was unspeakably cruel to Rebecca, so cruel that when Charles Gravely found her on the streets of Boston in 1853, she fell into his arms in tears. He had been the one she loved, so gentle and kind, and he fell in love with her all over again.

One day in February 1854, Jakob came home unexpectedly early in the afternoon and found Charles in his house with his wife. That's when he bestowed upon Charles a terrible thrashing and told Rebecca he would divorce her for adultery, and if she didn't admit her sins in court, he would find and kill Charles Gravely. So Rebecca testified in fear for her lover's life, but Charles wanted no more of Jakob and left Boston. After the trial and the divorce was finalized, Rebecca went to Charles' boarding house only to be told from the landlord that he had departed suddenly in the middle of February, but had left a note for her. "I love you, Rebecca, but even if Jakob divorces you, I'm afraid he would kill me if he found out where I was. I can't take that chance. Good-bye my love. Charles"

So he would never be coming back for Rebecca. That's when she went insane, and Jakob transported her to an asylum in Maine, and she changed her name to Jennie Gravely. Jennie eventually told Eva that Jakob was not her father and that a kind person named Charles Gravely was. In due time, I will complete this story.

Jack excitedly told Asha, "This is everything I need to show there was a divorce and that Eva was illegitimate. Could you please make me a copy of the court records and decision?"

Once Jack was back in his car, he called Anna and gave her the good news. "I'll show you the documents when I return to Minneapolis. It was the toughest genealogical search I have ever been involved in." Jack was back in a good mood and radiated his usual gregarious self. "How did things go for you in New York? Did you find Jimmy Gant?"

"Yes we did, but the case took an unexpected turn that I'll tell you about when we get together tonight at my place for Irish Stew and a Guinness or two. It's too complicated to cover by phone. When will you be here?"

"If I were superman, I'd be there in five minutes. By plane, it will be around 7 p.m. Will that work out for you?"

"It will work out perfectly for me, Jack. I'll be by the door at 7 p.m. with a hug and a kiss and a warm body." Jack started his car and burned rubber getting out of the parking lot of the Massachusetts State Archives.

CHAPTER ELEVEN

ANNA IN NEW YORK

The same week as Jack was grinding on as a genealogist in Boston, Anna, Tony, and Michael were active detectives in New York City, and I need to relate their endeavors also. How is that possible? Omnipresence is one of my more critical attributes. I myself, Time, am present at all times with all people, so when I was watching the battlefield of Gettysburg, I was also in the Louvre in Paris, on the Great Wall of China, and in deepest, darkest Africa.

Anna's plane landed at LaGuardia Airport in Queens and she, Tony, and Michael hired a taxi for a 23-minute ride, arriving during suppertime at their hotel in the Financial District of Lower Manhattan, a few blocks from Battery Park. When Tony Talridge had searched for Lower Manhattan hotels from Minneapolis, he had found this hotel had a government rate less than budget hotels in the same area. It wasn't comparable to Jack's hotel in Boston, but it was pleasant.

The first thing Anna did in her room was call Jack in Boston and tell him she had arrived safely. Then she rang up Tony and Michael for a team meeting over supper, where they agreed on a game plan to gather at 9 a.m. the next morning and walk over to Paul Boswell's address near Wall Street, a walk the concierge of the hotel said would be five minutes at most.

That evening before going to bed, Anna wrote in her journal:

"I just called Gramma McGrath, and I almost believe she is more excited about my renewed relationship with Jack than I am, if that's possible. She wondered if he had asked me to marry him yet, and I told her when he did I'd say yes in a snap of my fingers. It's interesting, when we were first dating four years ago, he was the one anxious to marry; now that's my desire. However, I'm not being fair to Jack. We both agreed to wait until we were out of the infatuation stage and into a mature love relationship – the difference between being excited when you first start reading a great novel and being filled and satisfied when you finish the last page. Jack and I are somewhere in the middle of the book, hopefully heading toward the last chapters.

"Tomorrow should be an interesting day. With a solid first step tomorrow morning on the road to finding Jimmy Gant, who knows but that we might be flying out tomorrow night with Jimmy in handcuffs."

The New York Monday morning weather was much like Boston – warm and pleasant enough to take a short jaunt outside. Michael O'Hara was his usual gleeful self at breakfast. "Visualize the picture of today before us, my friends. There are two people in Gotham City that'll be surprised as hell to see us arrive on their doorstep. We'll leave from here to pay Paul Boswell a friendly visit, he will blissfully tell us where Jimmy is living, and we'll surprise Jimmy and transport him back to Minneapolis kicking and screaming. It'll be a slam dunk." Michael had that impish grin on his face that meant he wasn't being serious.

Anna responded with her rendition of Irish sarcasm, a family trait she attempted to suppress for the most part. "No doubt, Michael, no doubt. Paul Boswell will be at his front door waiting for us to arrive, and once he realizes what a swell group of cops we are, he will willingly give us Jimmy's address, and the State of New York will graciously waive all extradition paperwork and let us haul Jimmy back to Minnesota this very evening."

"Exactly, Anna," exclaimed Michael, now laughing, "You see it clearly. Undoubtedly, it will be a piece of cake."

Tony Talridge did not share the sense of humor of his two Irish cohorts. "I'd suggest we stop fooling around and develop a *real* game plan to accomplish our mission. What if Paul is not at home? What if he refuses to tell us anything about Jimmy's whereabouts? How do we assure the New York Police Department is on board with what we are doing here?"

Anna turned serious. "Tony, thanks for bringing us back to the real world. Your questions are well put. To answer your last question, I talked to Lieutenant Daily as we left, and he said he'd contact the

Detective Bureau of the NYPD to request their help in obtaining extradition papers to speedily extricate Jimmy from New York. The lieutenant called me this morning with a contact name when we arrive at that point. If Paul is not home, we'll stake out his condo. If he clams up about Jimmy, we'll determine our options then. I have a few ideas."

The walk to Paul Boswell's condo on Wall Street, not far from Tiffany's, was less than five minutes. The manager of the building escorted them to the sixth floor and pointed out Paul's residence. Anna knocked on the door and announced, "We're from the Hennepin County Sheriff's Department in Minnesota, and we want to ask Paul Boswell some questions."

Paul answered the door. He worked out of his home as a very successful individual investor, after starting his career as a stock broker to the wealthy. He was a millionaire many times over, had been married three times with no children, and was between wives at the moment.

"To what do I owe this pleasure?" asked Paul, with anything but pleasure in his voice.

Anna responded. "Are you the Paul Boswell who graduated from Washburn High School in 1992?"

"I am."

"May we come in and ask you a few questions?"

"I expect it would not be wise of me to say no."

"It would not be wise of you," answered Tony.

Paul led them into the great room of his condo, with vaulted ceilings and a conference table used for business meetings.

Anna opened the conversation. "Mr. Boswell, we're not here because of anything you've done." Paul breathed a sigh of relief.

"Why are you here then?" asked Paul.

Tony responded, "We know an old high school friend of yours contacted you for help in finding a place to hide in New York City – Jimmy Gant." Tony was too direct, as usual. "A place to hide" could have been delivered softer with "a place to live." It might not have made a difference, but I saw Paul wince when Tony said "a place to hide."

"Jimmy called me from Minneapolis to see if I could find a place for him and his family to live in New York. I hadn't talked to Jimmy for over ten years, so it's not that we remained fast friends. Detective, you used the term 'a place to hide.' That's what I thought too. I suspected Jimmy was in some kind of trouble, and I didn't want to become involved in it. I told Jimmy he could call a real estate agent in New York to find housing. Jimmy was upset with me and slammed down the phone; I haven't heard from his since."

"Did you give him the name of an agent?" asked Michael.

"No."

Tony asked one more question. "Did Jimmy tell you why he wanted to live in New York City?"

"He didn't tell me, and I didn't ask him. Do you have any more questions for me?"

"Not at the moment," said Anna. "We may talk to you again in the next couple of days, so stay available. In the meantime, here's my card in case you hear from Jimmy or your memory suddenly recalls something you didn't tell us."

Once they were in the lobby of his building, Anna asked, "How do you assess Mr. Boswell's interview, gentlemen?"

"I think he was lying through his teeth," answered Michael.

"I concur," said Tony.

Anna weighed in, "That makes three of us. Now we face Tony's question, 'What do we do if Paul Boswell refuses to tell us anything regarding Jimmy's whereabouts?'"

Michael asked with a sly smile on his face, "What do you think Paul did the minute we left his place?"

"Called Jimmy to tell him we were in town and looking for him?" ventured Tony.

"I believe that's exactly what he did," agreed Anna. It's time for Plan B. I'll call my contact in the NYPD Detective Bureau and ask if he can help obtain a search warrant for Paul's cell phone and land line. Michael, would you go to City Hall and check on new utilities hookups during October 2010 to see if Jimmy Gant's name pops up? Tony, would you stake out Paul Boswell's condo on the sixth floor and trail him if he leaves? There's an alcove in the hallway you can hide in that's on the opposite side of the hallway from the elevators."

"Aren't you delighted you took me along now, ma'am?" said Michael with a twinkle in his eyes. I know where the New York City

Hall is – in Lower Manhattan, a few blocks from where we now stand. I also know that City Hall is not where I'd find utilities records. They would be in the Manhattan Municipal Building, near City Hall, a 40-story behemoth that's one of the largest governmental buildings in the world I'm told. I'm off."

"And I'll return to the sixth floor," said Tony, "and stake out Paul's condo."

And so they all departed for their various assignments. Michael was unsuccessful finding any listings for Jimmy Gant – I was in this very building when Jimmy reported his name as Alden Beaufort, to make it more difficult to trace him. Paul Boswell never left his place, so Tony spent a lonely eight hours in the alcove. Anna couldn't obtain a search warrant until late Tuesday afternoon for the phones of Paul Boswell. Even an NYPD contact could not accelerate the pace of accomplishing things in a metropolis like New York City, where the machinery of justice grinds slowly. The three detectives had been in contact throughout the day and agreed to meet in their hotel lobby at 6:30 p.m.

I will now bring you to a timeline in my past so you can listen to the conversation between Paul and Jimmy the minute Anna, Tony, and Michael left Paul's home. Paul used his land line to call Jimmy, just in case the detectives from Minnesota had the equipment to intercept a cell phone call.

Paul's adrenalin had spiked so dramatically that he was experiencing mild symptoms of stage fright. He inhaled and exhaled three deep breaths, which calmed him down enough to speak. "Jimmy, three detectives just left my home and are aiming to find you." Paul related to Jimmy the conversation he had with the detectives. "The lead detective is Anna Fitzgerald from the Hennepin County Sherriff's office, who looks more like a fashion model than a detective. I didn't give them *any* information, but I think it'll only be a matter of time before they find you. You'd best run for the hills."

Jimmy was calm on the other end of the line, tapping a pen on a tablet on his desk, and writing down the name Anna Fitzgerald. "I'm not about to run for the hills. I'm tired of being in hiding, and so are my wife and little Tessie. What will happen will happen. My consuming fear has been that Max Trevino will send his goons to gun down me, Joyce, and Tessie right in our apartment. Maybe it's time to talk to the police about Max and put him behind bars. He's so much a bigger fish than I am – like a walleye to a shark - that I may be able to avoid prosecution and jail time if I turn state's evidence against him. Did Detective Fitzgerald leave her card behind?"

"Yes."

"What's her cell phone number? Maybe I'll save her the trouble of finding me."

Paul gave him the number. "I'd suggest you not call her right away. Talk it over with Joyce. Once you commit to turning over evidence about Max, he'll be more intentional about killing you and your family."

"That's what I want to talk about with the detectives. Max will eventually find me and kill me anyway because I know too much about his dealings, and he no doubt figures I kept records of my operation that I turned over to him, which I did. I could hand over to the prosecution enough evidence and information to put him in jail for a long, long time, maybe a lifetime, if they can substantiate some of the killings I know he orchestrated. But I'll take your advice and think it over."

Anna, Tony, and Michael stayed in their hotel for supper, recapping their luckless outcomes of the day; the only bright spot being the upcoming search warrant for Paul's phones Tuesday afternoon, banking on his likely call to Jimmy.

Anna proposed the next day's assignments. "I'll visit my detective counterpart at the NYPD to see if we can speed up the search warrant. Michael, Jimmy probably put the utilities and where he's staying in a different name; that's what I'd do. Could you rifle through the files again and check if there is a Jimmy or James as a first name and something like Gant for a last name, just in case Jimmy's not creative. Tony, would you visit Mr. Boswell tomorrow morning and see if you can drag some information out of him; threaten him with obstructing justice if you have to. Maybe he was uptight yesterday because there were three of us. Then stake out his condo again to see if he visits our friend Jimmy.

After supper, Anna went straight to her room and pulled out a book she had taken along – *Lincoln* by Gore Vidal, a historical fiction rendition of Lincoln's presidency, one of the finest of that genre.

Four chapters later, Jack called and they related their adventures for the day, none of which could be called satisfactory. Jack read the poem he had written his first night in Boston to Anna, and she sat on the couch with tears in her eyes. After they hung up, Anna didn't go back to her book but remained on the couch staring straight ahead. "How loving of Jack to write a poem to me! He said it was the first poem he'd ever written; I hope it's not the last. It's fortunate he's not sitting here beside me; I don't think I'd be able to control myself."

Tuesday morning, the detective trio met for breakfast again before tackling their assignments. Michael was as luckless as yesterday because Jimmy Gant was more creative with names than Anna thought. Tony knocked on Paul's door again, and it was like talking to the Great Sphinx of Giza, followed by eight quiet hours in the alcove. Even threatening him with obstruction of justice did not loosen him up. Anna visited her detective counterpart to speed up the warrant but ran headlong into a detour. Instead of obtaining a search warrant that afternoon, it wouldn't happen until Wednesday. The judge who would have signed the warrant had the poor timing to die of a massive heart attack at breakfast and fell face first into his scrambled eggs.

That evening, Anna, Tony, and Michael met glumly for supper at a restaurant just off Wall Street. It didn't appear they'd be heading out of town anytime soon. At 6:45 p.m., Anna's cell phone rang. It was Jimmy Gant.

"I know you're looking for me, Detective Fitzgerald, and I'm ready to cooperate. Could you and your two fellow detectives come to my apartment on 15 W 31st Street in Midtown tomorrow morning at 9:00 a.m.? It's just south of the Empire State Building. I'm on the 28th floor, apartment 2814. Since my real name won't be on the directory downstairs or on the apartment door, look for Alden Beaufort and I'll ring you in."

Anna was too stunned to be loquacious. "Thank you for calling. We'll be there at the appointed time."

Anna related to Tony and Michael what Jimmy had said and then shook her head. "I don't understand that phone call. Jimmy obviously had talked to Paul and obtained my phone number, but why would he call and say he'd cooperate. Doesn't he know we're here to arrest him for masterminding the murder of his great uncle?"

Anna, Tony, and Michael would be in for a big surprise Wednesday morning, based on what I know.

"Welcome to our apartment, Detective Fitzgerald. This is my wife Joyce and my daughter Tessie. They'll be in a back room if you need to talk to Joyce."

"Thank you, Mr. Gant. These are my two fellow detectives – Tony Talridge and Michael O'Hara."

"I'm happy to meet all of you."

The three of them were stupefied. Why would a bad person and a murderer smile and invite them into his hiding place? It was like their purpose was to reminisce about old times in Minneapolis.

Michael broke the silence. "Why do you think we're here, Mr. Gant?"

"I think you found out Max Trevino took over my drug operation and you want to question me so you can get to him, but I disappeared, and you finally tracked me down. I'm tired of hiding and am willing to tell you everything I know."

The three detectives looked at each other with quizzical faces. Tony was the first to speak. "Um, actually, Mr. Gant, we're here to arrest you for planning the October 16 torture and execution of Eldridge Gant, your great uncle."

Jimmy's face turned the color of a white marble tomb and his voice went up an octave. "What? How can Eldridge be dead?" There was a short period of silence, as if Jimmy was processing what he just heard and thinking what to say next. He asked if he could walk to the kitchen to pour himself a glass of water. He needed time to frame the issue for himself, I would guess. When he returned, he gulped down half the glass and started his rendition of the story.

"I admit I'd planned to have two acquaintances rough up Eldridge to find out where he stored a tin box filled with Civil War coins worth over a million dollars, but I didn't tell them to kill him. Then I contacted Toby to call the job off because I was in fear for my life and my family's from Max Trevino's hit men. Toby was upset about not receiving the $5,000 I was going to pay the two of them before the job and said I owed them at least that. I agreed and gave $5,000 to my father before I left town to pay off Toby and Mack. Two weeks after I arrived in New York with my family, I had what I'd call a great awakening. My wife Joyce had left me a year ago to hide in Madison with our daughter Tessie because she lived in constant fear in Minneapolis with the roughness of my drug operation. After Max kidnapped Tessie and threatened to kill her if I didn't hand over my whole operation to him, I was out of the drug business and in this apartment with Joyce and Tessie."

Jimmy was talking fast and assumed the detectives knew more than they did about his dealings with Max, but their focus was on Eldridge's murder, so they didn't ask follow-up questions about the details of Jimmy's dope ring or Max Trevino. I'll fill you in later.

"I was at peace for the first time in my life when I realized my family was more important to me than being a successful criminal. I tried to call Toby to tell him his visit to Eldridge's was off forever; yet I'd still give him the second $5,000 of our agreement because that's what I'd promised them, but his cell phone number had been discontinued. So how was it that Eldridge was killed?"

"Hm," said Anna, and she told Jimmy about Toby and Mack, the night of the murder, and their new residence in the Hennepin County Jail.

"Did they just do it on their own, then?" asked Jimmy.

"From the information I have from your father and Mack, the answer to your question is no," replied Anna. "If you weren't the one who arranged the torture and killing, who was? Did you tell your father you were planning on killing your great uncle?"

"I told him I had hired two people to get the tin box from Eldridge the night I gave him $5,000 to pass on to Toby when Toby called him.

I never said I was planning on killing Eldridge. How did that come into the equation?"

Anna slipped into her staccato questioning style. "Mack Freighter told us your father Lucius *did* give Toby the $5,000 and also informed him he was acting as your agent. Lucius directed them to go ahead with torturing Eldridge to find out where the tin box was hidden and then kill him, and Lucius would pay them the other $5,000 when the job was completed. Did you give your father another $5,000?"

"Absolutely not, and I never knew Eldridge was killed. I didn't hear from Toby or Mack, which is obvious to me now, because they were in jail."

"Lucius told me he was afraid you'd do something rash when you started questioning him about the hidden coins, and Mack fingered you as the one who was behind the murder."

"I told you I had nothing to do with it." Jimmy's voice was firm and confident but cracking at the edges.

"Are you the one who had Toby and Mack lawyered up with your brother Jacob?"

"No! For what reason? I didn't even know they were in prison and had gone through with an attack on Eldridge or were told to kill him."

"Have you talked to Jacob since you left town?"

"No. I also hadn't talked to Jacob for a month before I left town. He told me his wife wanted him to stop protecting me from the police. She was afraid he might end up in jail."

"Then who had Jacob visit the two of them?"

A knowing look came on Jimmy's face. "There is only one person who knew enough to make the arrangements with Toby and Mack and have Jacob represent them?"

"And who would that be, Jimmy?" asked Anna with a voice that indicated she already knew what his answer would be.

"I hate to say it, but my dad. On my way out of Minneapolis, I stopped by his house and confessed to him that I had hired Toby and Mack to rough up Eldridge until he told them where the tin box was hidden, but had changed my mind and was going into hiding to protect myself and my family from Max Trevino."

"What was your father's reaction to your confession?"

"He looked taken aback, surprised, and asked if I told Toby the contract was absolutely off. I told him that in my last conversation with Toby I said the contract was on hold so he didn't get too upset. But the whole thing was off as far as I was concerned. I was in enough trouble already without having someone beaten up, and I never would have had my great uncle murdered. Even in my drug operation, I never had anyone murdered."

"Did you mention to your father you were heading to New York?"

"I told him I was in big trouble because of my drug operation and needed to pick up Joyce and Tessie in Madison and find a place to hide that would be difficult for anyone to trace."

"And you didn't reveal to him you were escaping to New York?" Anna had just asked Jimmy that same question, but part of her interrogation strategy was to ask the same question more than once if she suspected the person she was questioning was not telling the truth. Sometimes it worked, sometimes it didn't.

"No, I told him it would be best he not know; then he wouldn't have to lie for me."

Anna mumbled under her breath, "At least that part of the story coincides with what Lucius told me." Anna stared at Jimmy with her look that cuts into a person like a laser. "Continue on with what happened that night you visited your father."

"I had called Toby and left a message for him that the deal was on hold, and he quickly called me back, insisting that I owed him at least the first $5,000. I agreed and handed the money to my father and told him Toby would be calling him to collect it. I also told my father the coins were worth at least a million dollars and probably much more. I had a hard time explaining the coins were worth more than $1,450, but he finally caught on."

Anna was quick with another question. She was using information she had gathered from Lucius and Mack to see what did and didn't match up with Jimmy's side of the story. "Mack told me Lucius was acting as your agent, they were to execute the deal, and Lucius would give them the second $5,000 when they gave him the tin box. Did you give your father the second $5,000?" Again, she asked the same question to see if she could trip him up.

"I told you I never gave my father another $5,000. I told him as far as I was concerned, the deal was off. He made the arrangements to kill his uncle on his own, but why? Eldridge was 96 years old and my father would get everything of his anyway, including the tin box, and he already knew where that was. It doesn't make sense why my father would have Eldridge killed, but that's what he must have done."

"So, it's your word against your father's and Mack's. That's two against one. How do I know who's telling the truth? Knowing your criminal background and the gentleness of Lucius, right now I'd believe him over you."

"The gentleness of my father? Ask Jacob about that. My father had two personalities. To the outside world he acted as if he wouldn't hurt a flea. To Jacob and me, he was brutal, beat us for no reason, and told us how worthless we were. When each of us graduated from high school, we were on our own. Jacob went to law school; I became mixed up with drugs. It was almost ten years later that we talked to him again, after we found out he was suffering from mild dementia that transformed him into an amiable old man, and we accepted him back. I don't know what happened at birth, but our father was never very smart. I think that's what made him mean. He didn't like that Jacob and I were smarter than he was."

Anna was puzzled. Here was the man they had pursued with keen resolve to arrest and bring back to Minneapolis, and now she was wavering on whether they had the right person. "I will be questioning your father again when we return. In the meantime, we'll have to arrest you and extradite you back to Minnesota."

Jimmy calmly said, "You won't have to extradite me. I'll volunteer to return, if you'll offer me protection from Max Trevino. As to questioning my father, I suggest you question the two of us together, so he'll think twice about lying to you again. Then, once I'm off your list for killing Eldridge, we can discuss what I know about Max."

And so they all returned to Minneapolis mid-afternoon, Jimmy was put in protective custody, and Anna, Jimmy, and Lucius were scheduled for an interrogation session Thursday morning downtown. Anna had called Lucius and said she would arrange for a deputy to pick him up at his home at 8:00 sharp tomorrow morning. She strategically withheld the information that Jimmy would be in the same interrogation room.

It's time for the background of Jimmy I promised, so you'll better be able to interpret the interrogation tomorrow.

Jimmy, 31 years old, had gotten a girl named Joyce pregnant when he was 27. Though he was a gangster, he was a practicing Catholic and confessed to his parish priest his faux pas with Joyce, whereby the priest said, "Jimmy, you have an obligation to marry that girl or I cannot forgive your sin." And so Jimmy married Joyce. Personally, I was baffled that Jimmy would confess a sexual sin but leave untouched that he was a gangster selling drugs to people whose lives went downhill on a steep decline after they became steady customers.

When Tessie was born, Jimmy developed a soft spot in his heart for the little girl, the first softness I had ever observed in him. He was making headway as a family man, but his first love was yet his drug business, which he had fought hard to establish and protect. Three years after their marriage, Joyce took Tessie with her to her hometown of Madison, Wisconsin. She couldn't cope with Jimmy running a dope ring and being in constant warfare with other dope ring number ones, which is what the police call the heads of drug operations. Jimmy was extremely careful to protect himself, short of murdering anyone, but he was nearly killed three times during those first three years of marriage. Joyce still loved him, and Jimmy went to Madison as often as he could to visit Joyce and Tessie and supply them with everything they needed.

Before the contract with Toby and Mack was put into motion, an opposing number one, Max Trevino, found out Jimmy's family was in Madison and kidnapped Tessie, with a promise to Jimmy that his little daughter would be killed unless Jimmy turned his dope ring over to Max, whose own operation was five times larger than Jimmy's. Jimmy needed no time to think it over, turned all his records over to Max, vowed he would stay out of drugs in Minneapolis, and Tessie was returned to him in a quid pro quo exchange. The day after the exchange, Max sent his thugs to kill Jimmy because he knew too much about Max, which was thwarted when Jimmy went to New York to hide. Max was not as clever as Anna Fitzgerald, and he had not found Jimmy *yet* – but one day he would.

As Jimmy told Anna, being free of crime and drugs gave him a peace he had never known before. He told Joyce he was going straight and would be joining Paul Boswell in investments, but he'd first need to turn state's evidence against Max Trevino to get him behind bars and protect all of them for the long term.

Was Jimmy telling the truth about the murder of Eldridge Gant or was Lucius? Anna didn't seem to know for sure, but I do. There are a few surprises yet to come, and they should manifest themselves when Anna, Jimmy, and Lucius are in the same room.

Anna talked to Jack that night. He was surprised she was back in Minneapolis already. Sensing Jack's lack of progress had him feeling low enough to eat off a curb, Anna fought her excitement to tell the story of finding Jimmy and the surprising turn of events. She spent their phone time encouraging him to persevere. That night she wrote in her diary, "I feel so sorry for Jack; I wish I were there for him…I'm curious what tomorrow will bring with Jimmy and Lucius. I was so sure Jimmy was the mastermind behind the murder; now I have doubts. I hope tomorrow is the defining day."

CHAPTER TWELVE

WHO ARRANGED THE MURDER OF ELDRIDGE GANT?

Thursday morning, January 11, arrived with a bang for Lucius Gant. He had slept like a man awaiting execution the next morning; he tossed and turned all night and periodically spoke out in the night, "Why does Detective Fitzgerald want to talk to me again tomorrow?" It was a sorry sight.

Finally he fell asleep just as there was a bang on the front door at 8:00 a.m.; it was the deputy assigned to Rockford who was there to transport Lucius to the sixth floor interrogation room of the Hennepin County Sheriff's Office Investigative Division. The trip into downtown Minneapolis was traveled in total silence.

The deputy escorted Lucius into a small interrogation room packed with electronics and populated by Anna Fitzgerald and Jimmy Gant. When Lucius saw Jimmy, his face turned ashen.

"Hh…hello Jimmy. Wh…what are you doing here? I thought you was in hiding someplace."

"I'm through hiding, Dad. I need to get things straightened out in my life, and this is part of the straightening out. I won't say any more. This is Detective Fitzgerald's party."

Anna stood up as Jimmy and Lucius remained seated. She was wearing a blue blazer, grey dress slacks, and a crimson blouse. Standing there with her .40 caliber Smith & Wesson M&P semi-automatic handgun on the front of her belt and a pair of handcuffs on the back, she was an imposing figure.

Anna made an opening statement like a prosecuting attorney at a criminal trial. "Gentlemen, we're here to determine which one of you arranged the murder of Eldridge Gant. Lucius, you said Jimmy must have made the arrangements but never told you anything about it. Is that correct?" Lucius nodded his head, his face starting to build up with beads of sweat.

"Mack Freighter told me Jimmy was the arranger and you, Lucius, were the agent for Jimmy." Jimmy was about to say something, but Anna stared him down. She was not looking for an interruption to her review of the facts.

"Jimmy said he told you he had authorized a contract to rough up Eldridge until he revealed where the tin box was but mentioned nothing about killing him, further told you that he would never execute the contract, and gave you $5,000 to give to Toby when he called you. Is that correct, Jimmy?" Jimmy nodded his head; he now knew this was not the time for him to say anything.

Anna continued. "Mack informed me that you, Lucius, said you'd give him the other $5,000 when they gave you the tin box and they were now supposed to kill Eldridge. But Jimmy said he never gave you another $5,000. These statements can't all be true. There are a hell of a lot of lies being advanced, and none of us will leave this building until we separate the lies from the truth." Lucius' face was no longer sweating but had turned as pale as death.

Jimmy and Lucius had remained silent while Anna made her opening statement, but now the room was ablaze with accusations, denials, and counter accusations. Anna just let them have at each other until chaos took over. Jimmy had the upper hand in the arguing because Lucius had not fully grasped the rather complicated dissertation Anna had made. His mind could not keep up.

Anna screamed, "Stop!" so loud that it took both Lucius and Jimmy aback, as if someone had hit the pause button on a DVD and they were in suspended animation. "Gentlemen, these were only preliminary comments so you both know exactly the evidence I have. You will now go into separate interrogation rooms, and I will individually question each of you."

I gazed at the three of them. Anna was bold and on top of her game. Lucius had a face that looked like many I've seen in coffins. Jimmy was chewing his fingernails and looking nervous and worried.

I'm usually a rather passive observer, but I have to admit I was eager to see the outcome of all this.

Anna called Sylvia to bring Jimmy to the other interrogation room just down the hall.

Anna took a deep breath and started pounding Lucius with questions that didn't give him time to think or recollect what he had previously said. This was her technique to confuse those who were trying to cover up a lie, as well as to ask her subtle trapping questions.

"Lucius, the last time we met, at your house, you declared to me that Jimmy never told you about his plans to have your uncle killed. Do you want to stay with statement?"

"Y…yes." Lucius was at a formidable disadvantage with rapid questioning, sort of like a grade school team playing football against a college team.

"Jimmy said he gave you $5,000 to deliver to Toby when he visited you on his way out of town."

"Th…that's a lie." Beads of sweat were forming on Lucius' forehead again, and he was having trouble breathing.

"Mack's account to me was that you gave Toby the $5,000 and promised another $5,000 when you received the tin box and Eldridge was wiped off the face of this earth. What've you to say about that?"

"He's a l…liar."

"Why would he lie?"

"I d…don't know. Why d…don't you ask him?"

"I'll stop right here. You think about things while I talk with your son." Anna left the room and Lucius remained, clearly worried about what Jimmy would say and what Mack had said.

Anna now confronted a Jimmy who had lost much of his bravado and calm.

"Jimmy, you said you gave $5,000 to Lucius to give to Toby. Is there any way you can prove that, like removing such an amount from a bank account that day?"

"No," said Jimmy. "I used to carry at least that amount of money with me in cash all the time." Jimmy had a look on his face that seemed to say, "This is not going well."

"Did you give your father another $5,000 for after the tin box was obtained and Eldridge killed?"

"No, why would I do that if I had nixed the contract?"

"Why would Mack think you were the one behind the payments and Lucius was acting as your agent?"

"Because that's what Dad told him, I expect. Mack didn't have the real story, only my Dad's version of it."

"Hm," said Anna. "Jimmy, you said you gave $5,000 to your father and Mack corroborates that he and Toby received the $5,000 and were promised another $5,000 when the contract was completed. You say you didn't give a second $5,000 to your father. Is there any way you can prove that?" Anna must have asked that question to throw Jimmy off balance, because that's exactly what happened.

Jimmy was becoming angry now. "How can I possibly prove I didn't give him the money? Do I have to defend myself against a fabrication? That's not possible."

"Let's leave things there while I go back and question your father." Jimmy was still fuming when Anna left the room.

Anna returned to Lucius' room. "Lucius, you're not in a good place on the wheel of fortune." Lucius looked blankly at her; he was not good at seeing metaphors. "Mack said you told Toby you were acting as Jimmy's agent in transferring an initial $5,000 to him and promising another $5,000 when you received the tin box and Eldridge was dead. Yet you state you received no information from your son that there was a contract out on your uncle and he said he gave you no second $5,000 to give to Toby. Something is missing here, Lucius. What is it?"

I could almost hear the worn-down cogs in Lucius' mind grinding as they had never ground before. He became oblivious to where he was, and remained silent for more than a minute, while Anna watched him holding his head with his hands, his arms on his knees, and eyes closed. When he finally lifted his head and looked at Anna, the beads of sweat were gone from his forehead and a look of tranquility was on his face and he was barely stammering.

"Detective Fitzgerald, I love my son and wanted to p...protect him." He looked up at her with a pleading face. "On the night he left for Madison, Jimmy gave me $5,000 and told me Toby would call to get it. He said he'd get another $5,000 to T...Toby when he got the tin box in his hands and Eldridge was gone." Lucius paused and wiped his mouth. Anna looked at him impassively, but I could see her mind was racing with this new twist.

"Jimmy told me he'd fly to M...Minneapolis to get the box from me and then pay off Toby and Mack. And he told me something I didn't know. The coins I thought were worth $1,450 were really worth more than a m...million dollars." Why Lucius gave Anna that last statement, I don't know. It certainly didn't help his case, but he probably didn't realize that.

Lucius shook his head like he was trying to wake himself up and continued. "I wasn't happy a...b...bout my uncle being tortured and killed, but he was 96 years old and done lived a full life. D...Detective, I loved my son more than I loved my uncle. M...Mack was right; I took on being Jimmy's agent."

"Let's stop there, Lucius, while I talk to Jimmy about what you just told me."

Lucius looked nervous. "H...He'll just tell you I'm l...lyin, but I'm n...not."

When Anna informed Jimmy about Lucius' new accusation, his face turned red and his anger was a seething cauldron. "That man is so full of lies that he wouldn't know the truth if it hit him in the face. How can I defend myself against lies? It's his word and Mack's against mine."

I could see by the look on Anna's face that she was still shell-shocked with the bomb Lucius had exploded before her and was not able to continue questioning either Lucius or Jimmy. She stood looking at Jimmy, when a light came into her eyes. I had seen that happen many times in her short career: she had a brilliant idea.

She called for Sylvia to bring Lucius into the interrogation room she occupied with Jimmy.

Anna stood over them in a power position. "Well, gentlemen, we're at a standstill. Lucius said he was trying to protect you Jimmy, and you say Lucius is lying. Here's what we're about to do." Anna smiled and Lucius and Jimmy had quizzical looks on their faces.

"I'll leave both of you in this room and let you talk it out. When you are ready to present me with the truth, knock on the door and I'll come back in. I'm ready to stay here all day and night if need be."

Anna found Tony Talridge, Sylvia Johnson, and Joe Wilshire in their cubicles and asked if they could join her and watch the video and audio that Anna left running in the room Lucius and Jimmy were in. It was quite a scene. Jimmy was yelling at his father and pleading with him to tell the truth. Lucius told Jimmy he was telling the truth. They yelled and swore at each other for several minutes, and then became quiet.

Anna recounted to Tony, Sylvia, and Joe what had just occurred in the interrogation rooms and sought their advice for her return with Jimmy and Lucius in case they didn't come to a resolution locked together in one room. Tony was first to speak, "Lucius claimed Jimmy was ready to give the second $5,000 to Toby and Mack; Jimmy said he had nixed the deal. Mack mentioned the second $5,000 that Lucius said he'd give Toby and him when they delivered the tin box to Lucius after they killed Eldridge. Let's just say Jimmy is right – that he gave Lucius only the first $5,000. That means Lucius had to come up with the second $5,000." Tony stopped talking, but he had a "proud as a peacock" look on his face. Anna raised her eyebrows and puckered her mouth to indicate she thought Toby had a great idea.

Sylvia pulled on her right ear lobe, a habit of hers when she was in concurrence with an idea, and added, "We need to check Lucius' bank transactions to see if there is a $5,000 withdrawal on or before October 16. If there is, Lucius will melt under the evidence. If there isn't, the spinning arrow points to Jimmy."

"Right," said Tony, as if he had been about to say the same thing.

"Now, how are we to obtain that information by this afternoon?" asked Anna, with her hands on her hips.

Joe was caught up in the plan, as he rubbed his hands together. "First we need to find out what bank Lucius uses." Anna nodded in agreement.

"I'll pull him out of the room with Jimmy and quickly ask him in the hallway before he has a chance to think," said Anna, and so she did, and returned in two minutes with the answer. "I kind of tricked Lucius," she said with a smile. "I told him that if his story is true the coins would belong to him and we'd need to know what bank to transfer them to for safety. He gave me the name of the bank without thinking what other reasons I might have in asking him that question."

Anna gave them the name of a small bank ten miles from Rockford. "But how are we going to obtain financial information from that bank in a matter of a few hours?"

Joe had a smirk on his face and then started laughing quietly. "Our deputy in Rockford is married to the daughter of a bank president. Guess which bank?"

"No!" Anna exclaimed. "Did we finally get a break in this case? Joe, can you contact that deputy and have him talk to his father-in-law. You know what to have him ask."

"I do," said Joe. "I'll contact him immediately and tell him we need the information by this afternoon," and quickly left the room.

Meanwhile on the live recording of the interrogation room, Jimmy demanded that Lucius reveal to him why Anna had asked him out of the room. "I ain't going to tell you," said Lucius, and so commenced the yelling and swearing again. Finally, Lucius responded to Jimmy's harangue. "She t…told me she thought m…my story was the t…truth and wanted to know what b…bank I used so she could transfer the Civil War coins into my account." I think Lucius had meant to put Jimmy on the defensive, but his statement didn't have that effect.

Jimmy was smiling. "She was trying to trick you, Dad, into revealing your bank. It will be interesting to see why she did that, won't it?" Jimmy looked smug. Lucius looked confused.

That's all Jimmy said, and Lucius became silent again with a worried look that seemed to be asking, "Was I tricked?" Things were becoming interesting in the interrogation room. I knew what was in that bank account but I was intrigued to know how Jimmy and Lucius would respond to the information.

Two hours of silence later, Anna returned to the interrogation room. "Well, do you have things resolved yet? You've been quiet in here for quite some time."

"How do you know that, Detective?" said Lucius.

Jimmy answered his question. "Because they've been recording us in this room since Detective Fitzgerald left."

Lucius looked like someone who just had a large camera flash go off in his face. "Is th…that true, D…Detective?"

"I'm afraid it is, Lucius. Do you remember everything you said?"

"N…no, I d…don't." Lucius looked stunned, and I could hear those cogs squeaking again as if to say, "What did I say that could hurt me?"

"How about you, Jimmy? Do you have anything new to tell me?"

"As a matter of fact I do, Detective Fitzgerald. I just remembered something while we were sitting in this silent room."

"And what was that?" asked Anna.

"Have you gone through my cell phone that you took from me before you put me in this room?"

"No, we haven't done that yet. Why?"

"Because there are two messages I'd like you and my dad to hear."

Anna called Sylvia and asked her to bring in Jimmy's cell phone. Lucius was clearly troubled.

Jimmy looked at Anna as she held his phone. "Click into my archived phone messages for two from Toby on October 10 of last fall." Anna found the first one and played the message on speaker phone so everyone could hear it. Blaring out of the phone was an ugly message delivered by an ugly voice. Lucius was rattled; Jimmy had heard it before.

"Jimmy, you dirty rat. I've spent lotsa time with you on this. You can't just put it on hold and leave us high and dry. I'm looken for you to git $5,000 to me and Mack like you promised. We won't go through with visitin Eldridge until we hear from you, but you'd best come up with that $5,000 fast or somethin bad is gonna happen."

Jimmy added, "I was taken aback by how harsh that message was from someone I thought I had a good relationship with, and called Toby right back and talked to him live and told him his proposal was only fair, and I gave him my father's phone number to pick up the $5,000 I gave to Dad.

Anna found the second message that day from Toby and also played it on speaker phone.

"Jimmy, thanks for callin back. I been thinkin bout my phone message and how nasty it was. I was jist out a ma mind and took it out on a friend. I was still angry when you called and not grateful for your fairness. Sorry. I really appreshate you gettin us the $5,000 and understan we won't be goin through with the job till we hear from you.

I'll give your dad a call. I hope he wasn too hard on you when you told him bout our goin to roughen up Eldridge." Toby would only make that follow-up call because of his bond with Jimmy. He couldn't leave their relationship on a sour note.

Jimmy looked at his father, who was speechless, and then at Anna. "Well, Detective Fitzgerald, does that support what I've told you?"

I listened closely and could almost hear again the wheels whirring in Lucius' head as he rubbed his eyes in deep thought, and then spouted out, "Those phone messages don't prove n...nothin. H...how do we know Jimmy didn't call Toby later and t...tell him to follow through and he'd get the second $5,000?" I'm surprised Lucius was able to process all that and come up with such a proposition. That reminds me of an old Arkansas saying, "Even a blind pig finds an acorn sometime."

"There is that possibility, Lucius, but how do you explain that those messages conflict with Mack's story about your being an agent for Jimmy?"

"We'll m...maybe I didn't get my story exactly r...right," said Lucius. N...Now that I think of it, J...Jimmy did give me a second $5,000. H...How's he going to prove he d...didn't?"

"You're grasping for straws, Lucius. We checked with your bank and you took out a $5,000 mortgage on your house and asked for the money in cash. You're the one who had your uncle tortured and killed so you could get your hands on the coins. But why? You knew where the tin box was all the time and your uncle was 96 years old. Couldn't you just have waited until he died of natural causes, and you would have received all the money and the house without having to commit a crime?"

Lucius was trapped like an animal in a corner, but there was no fight left in him. He had had enough. It was a pitiful site to see him cowering in his chair and shaking like he was in below-zero weather in his underwear.

"I...I went for my an...nual physical in S...September and they ran a s...stress test on me. After some m...more tests, the doctor told me I had less than a y...year to live unless I had heart b...bypass surgery. Three artries were totally p...plugged and the f...fourth was gittin there. I have no health insurance, so when J...Jimmy told me the c...coins were worth more than a m...million dollars, I th...thought that was m...my only chance to live. Eldridge m...might live to be 100 years old. I d...didn't have that much t...time.

"I can't take the p...pressure anymore. It...It's k...killing me. I'm as good as d...dead one way or other. I was the one wh...who made the deal with Toby to get the b...box and k...kill Eldridge cause he told me he looked at the t...tin box at least once a week, and he'd th...think I was the one who stole em cause I was the only one who knew where the b...box was. But T...Toby and Mack screwed up the j...job and got c...caught. I th...thought it would be jist a matter of a couple weeks before I got the c...coins. Then you th...thought someone hired Toby and Mack, and I th...thought I'm 60 years old and would die in jail. J...Jimmy is younger and would have a life l...left when he got out of j...jail, so I led you to think it was him who d...done the planning."

"Thanks a lot, Dad," said Jimmy sarcastically. "I can't believe you threw your own son under a bus."

Lucius had nothing more to say. He sat there with his head between his hands, crying in bursts. He had no idea that a genealogical search was being conducted to find out who the coins belonged to before any will would be executed. He thought the will would be administered because his uncle was dead. That's as far as his brain would take him.

Lucius was handcuffed, arrested as a conspirator in the murder of Eldridge Gant, and taken across the street to jail. His confession would put him behind bars for 20 years. Jimmy went back into protective custody and started cooperating with the District Attorney's office to convict Max Trevino of drug running and murder. If that were successful, Jimmy would receive no jail time for turning state's evidence. That was the deal.

That evening Jack called Anna and told her he still had not uncovered the divorce. His voice sounded like it was coming out of a black cloud. Anna wisely withheld the information about her success in closing the murder case, listening to Jack and offering him encouragement. Seven times she told Jack how much she loved him and that's what was important, no matter what happened with the genealogical search.

Why, you may ask, didn't she share her success as an encouragement to Jack? I know the answer to that through observing people who are depressed. As they unburden their depression to another person, the last thing they want to hear is how great things are for someone else; they need encouragement and advice for their own condition. I could tell from the way Jack was acting and talking that he was in mild situational depression.

After she was off the phone with Jack, Anna sat down to write in her journal. "I learned an important lesson today. Don't come to a conclusion until you have all the facts. I had Jimmy as the culprit from the initial investigation and figured he disappeared because he didn't want to be caught for arranging the murder. I trusted Lucius too much because he seemed so vulnerable and harmless.

"So the murder is wrapped up, but the genealogical search is still up in the air. I pray that Jack has success tomorrow, and we can both celebrate Friday night. I'm on tippy toes waiting for him to come home. I never thought I'd miss anyone so much in my life, but he is such a huge part of my life that when he is gone part of me is gone."

CHAPTER THIRTEEN

THE STRANGE MATTER OF THE JOURNAL

At 7 p.m. Friday evening there was a soft knock on Anna's door, and she raced there so fast she tripped on the entry rug and slammed into the door with a thud. When she opened the door, there stood Jack with a concerned look on his face. "Are you all right, Anna? What was that thud?"

Anna didn't answer him with words. She grabbed him by the lapels of his open suitcoat and dragged him into her flat, closing the door behind them. Anna hugged him so closely he could feel her warm body through his shirt; then she kissed him so passionately it took his breath away. After two minutes of embracing and kissing, Anna replied, "I fell into the door hurrying to see you. Do you think I'm all right?"

"If you're not all right, I'd be crushed and not breathing if you were." Anna laughed, enjoying Jack's quick wit.

Anna walked with purpose to the refrigerator and pulled out two bottles of Guinness. Jack had deposited himself on the couch, and Anna sat so close beside him that they were thigh to thigh. The look on Jack's face was as if there was an electrical current going through his body. He put his arm around Anna's shoulders, and it was her turn to feel a current racing through her. My observation is that Anna saw there was a chance in this electrical storm that they may go too far and have to visit a confessional with a sin neither one of them wanted to commit. They were good Catholics.

"Jack, let's exchange stories of what happened in Boston and New York and here in Minneapolis, so we're both up to date." Jack looked relieved to hear the proposal, I would guess because he was so charged up he didn't know if he'd be able to control himself with Anna.

Jack led off. He recounted all the brick walls he encountered in Boston but his eventual success with everything he had hoped to find – Eva Meyer was the illegitimate child of Rebecca Jane Griffin and Charles Gravely, as attested to both in marriage and birth records and legal court records of the divorce of Jakob Meyer and Rebecca, which meant it was possible that Gertrude Ackerman was the only legitimate child of Jakob Meyer.

"We have all the legal documentation we need to show you are the only heir to Jakob Meyer's fortune, if Gertrude Ackerman was the daughter of Jakob Meyer and not Anton Schaar. Your Uncle Marv and I believe that is the case; but without hard, legal evidence, we are at a dead end."

Anna was next to the plate. She explained what had happened in New York, how Jimmy Gant had returned to Minneapolis voluntarily, and how Lucius Gant had confessed he was the one who arranged the torture and murder of Eldridge Gant. "That settles that part of the case," said Anna, "but we're only half way there – the genealogy part is still up in the air."

"I'm thrilled for you, Anna, to have completed the lengthy investigation of the crime and put everyone in jail who belongs there. Congratulations," which he punctuated with a kiss that was loving, but far removed from the heat of the love storm they had experienced earlier. "You are truly a clever and perseverant detective."

Anna returned his compliment with a kiss, also without the intensity of their earlier passion.

A buzzer went off on a crockpot in the kitchen, announcing the Irish Stew was done. "Let's eat, Jack."

Anna had orchestrated a romantic setting for supper – lit candles on the table, a subtle hint of light in the kitchen, soft music, a linen tablecloth of Shamrock green, and her mother's formal family-crest silverware.

With supper concluded, Jack fidgeted nervously and reached into his suitcoat for a jewelry box. Anna gasped.

When he opened the box, there was an emerald pendant surrounded by diamonds on a chain of white gold. Anna had a quizzical look in her eyes and cocked her head to one side.

Jack initiated what was obviously a rehearsed speech. "Anna, my darling, you know my parents came to this country directly from Ireland and raised me to be an Irish traditionalist. My father informed me last week that if I truly loved you, I should enter into a courtship with you as a first step to becoming engaged. I'm offering you this pendant to declare my love for you and asking you to be my love."

Anna took the pendant from Jack, put it around her neck, and put her right hand on Jack's right hand, with tears streaming down her cheeks. "I will be your girl, Jack, and wear this pendant every day as my declaration of love for you. But one thing bothers me, my love. Courtships usually last up to three years, and we're not teenagers. Did your father say anything about that?"

"He did, with the same words you just expressed, 'You two kids aren't teenagers anymore, so I think a courtship of about a year would be reasonable.'"

Anna loved Jack's father and respected him, and she knew Jack was not ruled by his father but highly regarded his advice. "If your father says a year, a year it will be, though I hope an engagement will come into our lives before that. I know you are the one I want to live with the rest of my life.

"My mother and her ancestors had a similar tradition; she and my father courted a year and a half before becoming engaged. I may be only 75% Irish, but tradition is important to me also. I won't pressure you to marry me before you feel comfortable doing so."

"Thank you, Anna, my darling. You are as precious to me as the emerald you will wear around your neck; no, more precious than that. You are the woman God meant me to share my life with." By this time, Jack had moist eyes.

Jack took Anna by the hand and led her into the living room, where they danced slowly, as if they were one, for an hour, saying nothing to each other, caught up in their own thoughts.

Then they went back to the couch, held hands, and talked until 2 a.m., when Jack became so tired he was almost sleeping sitting up. "I'd best head home and sleep in tomorrow to make up for the stress and sleepless nights in Boston."

"Will you call me tomorrow when you awake? I want to hear your voice."

"I will, but you'll not escape with only hearing my voice. A courtship means we'll spend the next year as close as yin and yang. I bought second-row tickets for "Cats" at the Orpheum from a friend who couldn't make the musical. We can dine at the Monte Carlo near your place. I made a reservation for 5 p.m. Is that all right with you?"

"It's perfect," said Anna, "I wouldn't change a thing."

In the three months following the courtship proposal, Anna and Jack were a couple who were together as often as the best of friends they were. Anna showed her pendant to her fellow detectives and received countless congratulations. Jack announced in his office that he and Anna were now formally a couple and received a large quantity of "best wishes" from one and all.

Jack and Anna periodically went to the History Center in St. Paul to try every avenue of finding a legal document for Gertrude Ackerman's birthdate that Jack and the genealogical guru in the Ronald M. Hubbs Microfilm Room knew about. They checked all the geographically pertinent newspapers in the microfilm room that were in existence from 1865 through 1868. They checked Gertrude's tombstone in St. Mary's Cemetery in Minneapolis. They visited government offices, historical societies, and libraries in Medina and Rockford. They went to the Wright County Historical Society and Heritage Center in Buffalo, Minnesota.

They found nothing but what Jack already knew – births in Minnesota were recorded nowhere else than churches until 1870. All their work to find any other document that proved the date of Gertrude's birth was like trying to find a certain rock on one mile of seashore, knowing that the certain rock may not even exist.

Ah, you are thinking, Time would know, and I do; but until yesterday, I didn't know if the great surprise would ever come to the surface. Let me give you a brief summary of what Anna and Jack had found out, and then I'll reveal the surprise.

The census dates were conflicting. Gertrude's birthdate on her death certificate was different from that on her tombstone. Her affidavit to recover Jakob Meyer's pension contained a birthdate that would make her Jakob's daughter, but that was information given by her and therefore not legal proof. No newspapers announced her birth; no historical books, like the History of Hennepin County 1881, gave ages of the children of Anton Schaar; no will or probate records were found for Jakob Meyer to document the birthdate of Gertrude; and all other searches wound up as dead ends. The only proof of her actual birth was in the church records of the Holy Name of Jesus Church in Medina, and they were consumed by fire in 1911 when the church burned down, or so it was thought.

I was there in 1911 and saw it all. On March 4, 1911, the rectory burned down via a kitchen stove fire. Immediately, a new rectory was built and completed a week before lightning struck the church June 3, 1911, at the base of the cross on the steeple, burning the church to the ground. Father Alphonse Goehring was the priest at the time.

Father Alphonse ran to the church when he heard the steeple bells ringing, calling for help, and removed the precious church records, which he stuffed into an unpacked trunk of his belongings in the front closet of the parsonage. He instantly raced back to the church to save the cross above the altar and the chalices that held the sacraments. He was found in the aisle of the church with those three items, dead from smoke and lack of oxygen.

On the day of his funeral, that large trunk in the front closet, with the church record books having slipped almost to the bottom in moving it to the front entryway, were given to his only brother and kept in the basement of that brother's house for 95 years.

Then, just yesterday, his twelve-year-old great-great-granddaughter Alice, still living in the same house, was bored from a weekend of rain and a Monday off from school and no one to play with. Tired of walking around the house, she decided to explore the dreaded old coal bin room that was dusty and dank and, from what she told her parents three years ago, a hiding place for who knows what horrible creatures. But twelve years of age brings about a new maturity and a new quest to discover the unknown.

She stepped cautiously into the coal bin, now a repository of all sorts of junk, and turned on her flashlight. There before her was the trunk given to Father Alphonse's brother, which had been kept in a corner of the basement, unopened, until the house obtained an oil-burning furnace, and then thrown into the coal bin and forgotten, its secrets secure – until that day. Alice, with her cute blonde hair speckled with dust, opened the trunk and threw out old clothes and pictures and carpenter tools, until she found something worth paying attention to – old books. She was mystified with what they were, so much like a phone book with dates to her, but all in German. She showed the books to her father, who knew enough German to instantly recognize them for what they were and called a stunned Father Jansen at Holy Name Church and took the record books to him that same evening.

Father Jansen was so overjoyed to recover the lost records that he fell to his knees and thanked God for His remarkable provision. While on his knees he remembered Anna's and Jack's visit last November and vowed he would call her the first thing in the morning.

Anna was at her desk at 9 a.m. on April 24 when the phone rang.

"Detective Fitzgerald, this is Father Jansen from Holy Name of Jesus Church in Medina. Do you remember when you and your boyfriend stopped by to see if the church records burned in the fire of 1911 may have been mysteriously found?"

"Yes, I remember you, Father Jansen," replied Anna. I don't think she had a clue what was coming next.

"Well, they *have* been mysteriously found, the church records that is." Father Jansen's voice was crackling with excitement, and Anna jumped out of her chair so fast that her fellow detectives nearby said later they thought she had been stung by the bee who was flying through the office area.

"Father Jansen! Am I dreaming or did you just tell me the church records from the fire of 1911 have been found?" Anna was practically shouting into the phone. This was rather odd behavior in the staid confines of a double string of detective cubicles.

"That's exactly the case. Would you like to see them?"

"Is the Pope a Catholic?" was Anna's hurried response; I thought she could be a bit more original than that. "Can I call my boyfriend?" asked Anna with a voice like someone experiencing stage fright. "If he's available, I'd like to drive out to Medina this afternoon. Will that work?"

"Yes, I'll be here all afternoon. I'd also suggest you bring someone who reads German, because that's the language used for recording vital statistics in the 1860s."

Anna immediately called Jack, who was free that afternoon. Teddy, one of Jack's law partners, had an undergraduate major in German and was the unofficial translator of all German language legal documents. He also was open that afternoon and willing to be their on-site translator.

At 2:14 p.m. Anna, Jack, and Teddy arrived at Holy Name and walked up to the parsonage. Father Jansen opened the door, and was pleasantly surprised when Anna greeted him with a big hug.

"I pray I deserve that hug by what you are going to find in the 'lost' church records," said Father Jansen.

"You deserve that hug because you called me so soon after you received the church records, whether we find what we need in them or not," responded Anna.

After a bit of small talk, Father Jansen brought them into his dining room, wherein lay the church records from 1857 to 1911 on the large table in the middle of the room. Jack separated out the book that contained records from 1866 to 1868. "Let's start with 1866," proposed Jack, "because that year holds the most promise for our theory of who belongs to whom. Teddy, could you sit down here and translate the German recordings for us?"

Teddy started with January 1, 1866, with the birth of Agnes Fredrickson. Not all days had recorded events, so Teddy quickly advanced to January 21, 1866, and there it was. "Here's your smoking gun, Jack," said Teddy with an emotion similar to the first man in California who discovered gold: "Gertrude Schaar, born to Anton Schaar and Elizabeth Meyer Schaar."

Anna clapped her hands in excitement. "We've solved the mystery. We know Anton married Elizabeth August 12, 1865, with Gertrude four months in the womb. That means she was conceived in April 1865 sometime, one month before Jakob was mysteriously murdered in his wood bin on May 24, 1865, and two months prior to Anton Schaar's first wife Barbara dying on June 14, 1865." Anna had a quick mind to calculate gestation benchmarks and a steel-trap memory to recollect the pertinent facts of the case. She continued with a prescription of what would happen now.

"We have the hard evidence we need to obtain a search warrant to exhume the bodies of Jakob, Gertrude, and Eva to check DNA samples, and put to rest the unlikely possibility that Anton had an affair with Elizabeth while he was still married to Barbara. Uncle Marv said Anton most likely didn't even know who Elizabeth was until Barbara died and then checked to see if any widows might be available for him to marry and raise his family."

I had never seen Anna so delighted over the facts of a case. She had learned much about genealogy in a short time, thanks to Uncle Marv, Jack, and her own curiosity about how genealogy searches were conducted.

"I know you are very excited, Anna," said Jack, "as I am, but I'd suggest we nail down the marriage date of Anton and Elizabeth in the record book that contains 1865, as another piece of evidence to show a judge." This was Jack's approach to lawyering – "bury them with evidence."

"Then we can look in the 1868 records to verify the birth date of Adolph Schaar, Gertrude's younger half-brother. If he's listed as being born in 1868, that will pile on more evidence that Gertrude was not born in 1868."

So Teddy went back to work briefly by looking in the records for August 12, 1865, and there it was: the marriage date of Anton Schaar and Elizabeth Meyer. Then he went to the records of 1868 and didn't have to go far to find Adolph's recorded birth of January 6, 1868.

"Father Jansen, may we borrow these records to show a judge and secure a search warrant to obtain DNA samples of Jakob and Gertrude?"

"Absolutely, my dear."

On May 2, 2007, Anna, Jack, and Teddy were in the chambers of Judge Amy Carmichael, Judicial District 4, Hennepin County, Minnesota. They took in all the evidence obtained from Marv Schaar in Buffalo, from Jack's trip to Boston, and from the Holy Name Church record books they had acquired from Father Jansen.

"I'm impressed by your thoroughness of information, both legal and otherwise, that heavily points to Jakob Meyer and Gertrude Ackerman being father and daughter and indicates that Eva Gant is not a daughter of Jakob Meyer. I'll grant you the search warrants you are requesting to exhume the three bodies and run DNA samples on them."

On May 10, Anna Fitzgerald stood by the now open grave of Gertrude Ackerman in St. Mary's Cemetery in South Minneapolis, as the Hennepin County Crime Lab obtained a DNA sample from her bones. On May 11, the same exercise took place at Elmwood Cemetery in Rockford for Jakob Meyer and Eva Gant. For this type of sample, a mitochondrial DNA is best suited, and this was performed on the two samples once back in the lab.

Anna remained behind when the crime lab left each site and before the bodies were buried again. "This is my great-grandmother," exclaimed Anna at the first site, and bowed her head in reverence and awe. "Her bones are all that are left behind; I wish I knew more about her than the bare genealogical outline of her life."

When she stood over the body of Jakob with head bowed, she said, "Great-great-grandfather Jakob, if you really are my great-great-grandfather, how did you obtain enough greenbacks to buy the Civil War coins? Who murdered you in 1865? Were you ever the rascal, or did you have redeeming qualities? I have seen your handwriting; now I have seen what is left of your body." She stood for a long time over the grave, until the time came to rebury the bones. She did not spend time at Eva's gravesite.

When the DNA results were given to Anna and two members of her Eldridge-Gant-murder team, Sylvia Johnson and Michael O'Hara, at the Hennepin County Sheriff's Crime Lab, she sighed in relief. The results showed that with the amount of DNA matching, it could be assumed beyond a reasonable doubt that Gertrude Ackerman was a daughter of Jakob Meyer and Eva Gant was not. A seven-month genealogical search, with many low points and some high points, had come to a conclusion.

"You see, Anna, my darling, the O'Hara luck was with you again," said Michael. "I had no doubt we'd find out who the coins belonged to and it would be you. We should go to an Irish pub and celebrate our accomplishment."

Michael O'Hara aggravated some people with his frivolous style – everything was the grist of his humor – but Anna found him amusing. "Oh, Michael, I am so glad you helped out Jack and me in our research. What was it again you did?" said Anna while laughing.

"Oh, I was ever the encourager," said Michael, "and of course the good luck charm. I'm afraid, Anna, your being only 75% Irish was not enough luck to bring you through this one."

"Well, how about Jack? He's 100% Irish."

"Well, there you have it. The case was so complicated it took the luck of two full-blooded Irishmen to bring about a favorable outcome."

Anna laughed again. "Oh, Michael, is there ever getting the best of you in an argument?" Michael lifted his arms up, shrugged his shoulders, lifted his eyebrows, and smiled.

When she returned to her office, Anna called Jack and gave him the good news. "In my wildest dreams, Jack, I never thought we'd reach this point."

"I've seen such things as this happen before," replied Jack, "but I must admit I had my doubts when we reached the ultimate brick wall of needing the church records from Holy Name Church, which had been burned to ashes in a fire. I thought something would pop up, but my hope dwindled, until I felt as if I were banking my future on winning the Powerball jackpot."

"Well, Jack, what happens now?"

"I'd like to tell you it will be simple to authenticate you as the sole heir of the coins, but nothing is simple within the legal realm. Jakob didn't have a will so we'll have to follow the intestate probate process. However, Jakob's note in *Fifteen Decisive Battles of the World* was addressed to his wife Elizabeth, explaining where the tin box was hidden, what was in it, and that it was Elizabeth's inheritance. That shows intent. And Jakob's note in *The Gentleman Farmer* is an indication he did not want Eva to inherit anything because she was illegitimate, which was legally proven when I was in Boston and confirmed with the DNA samples.

"Why don't we get together for supper at McGovern's Pub tonight, and I'll give you a brief dissertation on probate law in Minnesota as it relates to this case."

It was the evening of May 17, a low-cloud drizzly day that was a good complement to the unusual heat and humidity of the day before. McGovern's Pub was bustling at 6:30 p.m., but there was always a place for Jack and his friends.

Jack arrived first because it was a short drive from his office. Anna pulled in a few minutes later and walked in at exactly 6:30. When Anna reached their booth, Jack stood up to bestow on her a more-than-friends hug and a lingering kiss. I could almost feel the heat of the moment. Sweethearts that they were, they sat on the same side of the booth.

They each ordered one of the turkey specials and a pint of Guinness. Anna winked at Jack. "Well, my darling, since this is a business meeting on probate law, give me the Reader's Digest version for now, and I can ask for more details if I want."

Jack smiled back. "Well then, a business meeting it shall be. I made a copy of Minnesota Statute 524.2-803 for you. You'll note the title is 'Effect of Homicide on Intestate Succession, Wills, Joint Assets, Life Insurance and Beneficiary Designations.' Our issue is found under (a)."

"I can see that," said Anna. "It says Lucius can't inherit anything because he arranged for the murder of the decedent. However, 'the estate of the decedent passes as if the killer had predeceased the decedent.' Does that mean everything goes to Lucius' two sons, Jimmy and Jacob? Lucius told me Eldridge hated them. It would be a shame for them to get anything." Anna had a discouraged look on her face and put her head down.

"Don't get the razor blades out yet, Anna. It will be important to see what is in Eldridge's will. Given that he didn't like the children of his nephew, he may very well have written them out of the will – just in case." Anna smiled weakly and squeezed Jack's hand.

Jack squeezed back with a smile on his face, as if to say, "I've just started." Anna returned to a listening mode.

Jack continued. "Our first move would be to obtain a copy of the will. I can do that. If that is favorable, we would petition the Probate Court for a hearing on the ownership of the coins, with the evidence we used to obtain a search warrant to exhume the bodies of Jakob and Gertrude, as well as the note Jakob wrote to Elizabeth giving the coins to her and the note about Eva.

"That sounds better," said Anna, as she put her arm around Jack's waist.

Jack continued. "The court would proceed to 'discover' interested parties, which from your research in the murder would be only Jimmy and Jacob Gant. However, the court administrator would advertise in the Minneapolis StarTribune for two successive weeks to see if there are any other parties who might contest a Decree of Descent naming you as the only heir. The second advertisement would be ten days before the hearing, so we're talking about a month right there. Depending on whether Jimmy and Jacob contest your claim and whether any other claimants, legitimate or otherwise, come out of the woodwork, it could be up to a year or two before a Decree of Descent is issued to you and you receive the coins."

That was a complicated meal to digest, but Anna was as bright as those doctors who have mastered the gathering and processing of information. After all, she was a detective noted for her quick mind, fact-absorbing memory, and ability to frame an issue on the spot.

"What about the house?" asked Anna.

"That's possibly a different matter. Eldridge's line of descent owned that house since 1865, and it was not specifically stated in your great-great-grandfather's note to his wife in the *Fifteen Battles* book, before his death. Again, it will depend on what is stated in Eldridge's will."

"So be it," said Anna. "The whole matter of the coins can wait ten years for that matter, because I *will* give them away to a disabled veteran's charity."

Anna turned to Jack, smiled, put a hand on his shoulder, and kissed him. "Whatever would I do without you, Jack?"

That night before Anna went to bed, she wrote in her journal. "Solving the murder of Eldridge Gant was gratifying, but knowing my family tree is spine-tingling. Without the murder case, I would never have become involved in genealogy; and without the genealogy, I would have never become involved with Jack again.

"Now that I know who my great-grandmother and great-great-grandfather are, I'll seek Jack's help to trace my lineage back from Jakob. I'm only a novice genealogist, and I want to become as expert as Uncle Marv. I'll visit him this Saturday with Jack and tell him all that has happened. No doubt he'll be greatly excited! After tracing my father's lineage as far back as I can, I'll tackle my mother's, with Jack's help of course. This matter of genealogy has become a chronic affliction, I'm afraid.

"I now know I will be married to Jack eventually, and that gives me great comfort; but like the Decree of Descent, it will take time. I guess God wants me to learn patience.

"With one murder solved, a family tree proven, a love established, and an inheritance issue yet to be resolved, there seems to be another loose end that is not of consequence legally but is gnawing at my curiosity – who murdered my great-great-grandfather Jakob and why? How could I possibly find the denouement of a mystery that occurred in 1865, unless a miracle happened like the re-appearance of the church records? Maybe whoever murdered him might have written somewhere about his crime, and the diary or journal or note is lying someplace waiting to be discovered. Maybe."

CHAPTER FOURTEEN

THE MURDER OF JAKOB MEYER

Unfortunately for Anna, there *is* no diary or journal or note, or anything else for that matter that gives any insight into who killed Jakob Meyer or why. Only I, Time, know, for I was there in 1865 when it happened, watching with great interest, not knowing how the murder then would be tied into events taking place in 2006 and 2007.

Back in the chapter "Jack Quinn in Boston," I informed you Jakob's first wife, Rebecca Jane, told Eva that Jakob was not her father but that a man named Charles Gravely was. By this time, Rebecca, who had changed her name to Jennie Gravely, had been in the insane asylum in Augusta for nearly 11 years, in and out of lucidity on a random basis. In her madness, she went back in time to little Rebecca, six years old, and addressed trees as her parents and siblings when she was taken on walks by an asylum guard. In her more lucid moments, she displayed a murderous hatred for Jakob, which was her state of mind when she revealed to Eva who her real father was on Eva's fourteenth birthday on April 14, 1865.

Flashing back to past points on the linear path of history, I, Time, have seen many extraordinary circumstances, yet I am still intrigued by the unexpected. In 1854, Charles Gravely, in fear of being killed by Jakob in Boston, fled to the west and landed in St. Paul where he found a job in the Bureau of Land Management. He was a supervisor there in 1858 when Jakob Meyer came in to register the bounty land he had won in a poker game. Charles saw Jakob when he was checking the large customer service area through the blinds in his office, as he periodically did, but Jakob did not see Charles. Frozen in fear for several minutes until Jakob left, Charles cautiously left his office to talk to the clerk who had processed the registration.

"What was the name of that fellow you were just working with and what did he want?"

The clerk shook his head in disgust. "His name is Jakob Meyer and he registered a land bounty for 160 acres in the Rockford townsite. He was a most unpleasant man to work with."

"Why?" Charles queried hesitatingly, sweating throughout his body and gulping for air in his continuing fear.

"When I asked if he had a wife he barked at me, 'Why the hell you need to know that?' I told him we needed such information to put on a land deed."

Charles' fear turned to dread of what happened to the only woman he had ever loved and their child. "And what did he answer to that?"

"He said gruffly that he had a wife named Rebecca but divorced her and she was now living in an insane asylum in Augusta, Maine. I then asked if he had any children who should be noted on the registration. He barked at me again, 'What the hell you ask so many questions? I jist want to register the land.' I told him again that such information was needed to register the deed. He had a wild look in his eyes when he said, 'A girl came after the marriage, but she were a bastard and no daughter of mine. I don't want her on no deed!'"

Charles' emotions raced into high anxiety as he asked one more question. "Did Jakob say who the father was?"

"No, he just stared at me, like he was daring me to ask one more question. I didn't and he never said another word until the deed for the land was completed and registered. Then he left."

Charles breathed in deeply and then exhaled with a sigh of relief. He waited an hour to assure Jakob was far away, and walked to a nearby telegraph office, where he sent a question to the Augusta, Maine, City Hall as to the name and address of the asylum there. An hour later a messenger from the telegraph office brought Charles a return telegraph that had the information he needed.

Charles Gravely spent the next two hours composing a letter to Rebecca, tearing up copy after copy, until he had what he wanted. I was watching the whole time.

Dear Rebecca,

I have often wondered what happened to you since I left Boston for St. Paul, Minnesota, but I did not know how to contact you without my message being intercepted by your husband. I have missed you terribly and have desperately wanted to know what happened to our child. I have never married because no woman ever measured up to my love for you.

A fearful and wonderful thing happened to me this morning. Your ex-husband Jakob came into my building to register a plot of land in a townsite about fifty miles west of St. Paul. He did not see me. After he left, I talked to the clerk who waited on him, and his conversation with Jakob revealed that you were in an asylum in Augusta, but nothing was mentioned about our daughter.

If I came to Augusta, would I be able to arrange for your release from the asylum and meet my daughter (tell me about her; she must be about seven years old)? I love you so much. I found out you are divorced from Jakob. I know we could make it on our own with our daughter. Please write back to me and I'll be there within a couple of weeks.
Charles

I was a bit skeptical that Charles loved Rebecca as much as he stated in this letter. After all, he was the one who seduced her when she was very young, abandoned her and left her with his child, started up an affair again when she was a married woman, left her to the cruelty of Jakob, and wrote her a good-bye note as he fled Boston for Minnesota, which was the tipping point of Rebecca's descent into insanity. And now he claims his great love for her? There was nothing in what I have observed of Charles that indicated such a transformation had taken place, but like many others, he was so self-centered that he probably didn't think anything he did was wrong and said to himself that it was time to claim his first love again.

It took a month and a half before Rebecca was herself enough to write back to him, and she also had a short memory of what Charles had done to her and had been living in a fantasy world where he was her knight in shining armor.

My dear, dear Charles,
How wonderful to hear from you. I have talked to my parents and sisters, who live on the grounds of the asylum, about how I miss you and wish I could find out what happened to you. Now I know.

I think you would not know me now if you saw me. When I look in a mirror, I do not recognize myself. Jakob's cruelty took most of the lifeblood out of me, and when I went to the boarding house where you were living and read your note to me, the rest of my life flowed out and I became insane. They will never let me leave here, and I do not think I would want to. There is cruelty in the asylum, but I am treated kindly because I cause no trouble. I feel safe here.

We have a daughter, now seven years old I think, that I named Eva after my mother. She is so pretty, but I have not seen her for the last four years, or is it three years, I lose track of time. When she is old enough, I will tell her that the wonderful Charles Gravely is her true father, and how hateful my ex-husband Jakob was.
With all my love,
Rebecca Jennie Gravely

How Rebecca can state that Charles' note to her pushed her into insanity and still declare her love for him is evidence to support my belief that she was living in a fantasy world, one of the many symptoms of her madness.

Shifting forward to April 14, 1865, a mostly lucid Jennie Gravely (aka Rebecca Meyer) was talking to her daughter Eva, who now lived in Augusta, wanting to be close to her mother. "Oh, Eva, I am so happy you have moved here. Maybe this will help me get better." She had tears in her eyes.

Eva was not prepared for the forbidding nature of this asylum, clean but undoubtedly a place of confinement in so many ways, with guards everywhere; and she felt compassion for her mother, hugging her and speaking with pronounced passion, "Oh, I pray so, Mother; I pray so."

"You are so grown-up looking, Eva; you seem more like twenty than fourteen."

"It's been a hard life living with Uncle and working long hours at his store since I was seven. I feel like I *am* twenty years old. The only joy in my life happened on my tenth birthday, when Uncle bought me a gift of a share of a horse that lived on a farm just outside Boston, where I went every chance I had to ride her. I've become a real horsewoman in the last four years, Mother. It was hard to leave Ginger on that farm, never to feel her nose nuzzle my hand, never to ride her again," as tears welled up in Eva's eyes.

Eva's mother, on her own track of thinking, looked her daughter straight in the eyes and told her about her real father, Charles Gravely, and how wicked Jakob had been. Eva was shocked by the news that Jakob was not her father but happy in a way because he had abandoned her to her mother's uncle when she was three. Rebecca filled in the details of where Jakob and Charles were living and how she wished something terrible would happen to Jakob. Then, as suddenly as her sanity had come upon her, it abruptly left, and Rebecca lived in madness for the next month, unable to recognize anyone, communicating only to the trees on the grounds outside the asylum.

Though her mother was oblivious to the world around her, Eva held her right hand in both of hers. "If there is any way I can fulfill your wish, Mother, I will do so. I hate Jakob almost as much as you do for how he ruined your life and put you in this dreadful place."

On May 20, 1865, Eva entered the Bureau of Land Management in St. Paul soon after it opened and asked to see Charles Gravely. She was ushered into his office and announced to him that she was his daughter Eva. There was a moment of silence; Charles didn't seem to know what to do, but Eva did. She stiffly hugged her father.

"Oh, Eva, what a joy to see you! I've corresponded with your mother for the past seven years. During the first year, I asked twice if she wanted me to visit her and that I'd move to Augusta if she wanted." Charles opened a drawer in his desk and pulled out two letters from Rebecca. "The first answer was, 'I think it best you not see me as I now am, merely a dishrag of a person, my beauty spent, my mind unstable, my body ravaged by months at a time of not eating properly.'" Changing to the second letter, Charles read, "Dear Charles, please don't request coming here again. Let's remember ourselves as we once were, vibrant and deeply in love. I can live with that memory. I could not endure the look on your face if you saw me now."

Charles pulled out a handkerchief and wiped his eyes. "In the last letter I received from your mother, she told me you were coming to Augusta to be near her. She was so happy about that. But now you are here. Has something happened to your mother? Is she still alive?"

Eva was a complex person, and I sometimes wondered if she had inherited genes from her mother that would eventually drive *her* to insanity. You never knew for sure which personality was in control of Eva. The letters from her mother to Charles turned her face from calm and in control to blood red and radiating intense anger.

"I hate Jakob for what he did to Mother," cried Eva with a voice so grisly I didn't recognize it. "Yes, she's still alive," said Eva with the same harsh voice, "but her madness has taken over with an unrelenting intensity." Eva suddenly became calm again and spoke in a quiet voice. "She doesn't even know who I am. I thought this would be a good time to visit you and visit Jakob."

Charles looked shocked. "Why would you want to visit Jakob?"

"Let's just say I'm one who likes to complete pictures, and Jakob was a part of my life. I don't even know what I'll say to him when I meet him. I wish somehow I could cause him pain for what he did to Mother. I guess I'll think about that on the way there. Can you tell me, Father, how to get to Rockford?"

Father looked at daughter and daughter looked at father. There seemed a bond building between them even in such a short time.

"There are a couple of ways. You could travel by stagecoach on the territorial road that heads west from Minneapolis and goes through the townsite of Rockford or you could take a steamboat from St. Anthony Falls to the townsite of Monticello and then work your way down to Rockford. I'd suggest the territorial road. It's direct, well-travelled, and safe."

"Is it possible to go by horseback? I don't plan on staying long at Jakob's and don't want to be waiting for another stagecoach coming back the other way."

"I said it was safe to go the territorial road, but I would not extend that to a woman riding by horseback."

"I had anticipated that. The riding clothes I have are a man's outfit, what I wore to ride my horse in Boston. I dress like a man and I ride like a man. No one out there will ever suspect I'm a woman, with my hair gathered up under my hat."

"I guess you're going to do what you're going to do. If you left now, it would take you two days, and there are places you could stay along the way." Then Charles became quiet.

Eva could see Charles was concerned about her visiting Jakob. "Don't worry, Father, I won't tell him anything about you. That will be our secret."

Charles let out a sigh and became more relaxed. "That's exactly what I was worrying about. I don't trust Jakob. If he knew I was here, he might kill me. He's a brutal man. By the way, I have a friend on the western edge of Minneapolis who would lend you a horse to make your journey. I'll draw you a map of how to find his place, I'll give you a note to hand to him, and I'll draw a map of how to get to Jakob's place."

You may think this was chiefly a business-like interaction between father and daughter, and it was, but both Charles and Eva were matter-of-fact people cut out of the same bolt of cloth, dealing with practical matters first. Once those were taken care of, Eva and Charles talked for nearly an hour in his office, catching up on each other's life, coming a little closer to the father-daughter relationship that had been denied them for so many years. Eva said she'd stop to visit Charles on her way back to Augusta.

It was mid-afternoon May 22, 1865, when Eva rode her horse to the rear of Jakob's house. He had the lid open to the wood bin attached to the back of the house and was throwing a few short logs into the bottom. The top of the bin was at ground level, covered with a heavy, angled lid on which were nailed the same shingles that were on the roof; Jakob had dug the shaft down four feet square and eight feet deep, which was nearly empty now that winter had run its course.

Jakob turned abruptly to see a young woman (Eva had taken her hat off and let her hair fall down) sitting atop a roan-colored mare. He scratched his head. "Who are you and what you want?" said Jakob in a gruff voice. If he were graded for social interaction and genteel communication skills, he would receive a low F.

"I am Eva Meyer from Boston. You and my mother raised me for three years before you brought her to Maine and deposited me with her Uncle and Aunt in Boston." Eva had no emotion in her voice. It was as if she were giving a speech on trees in a classroom. "And I'm here because I want to make contact with all the people who have been a part of my life. I won't stay long."

Jakob stood stupefied and then turned angry. "You damn right you won't stay long. Git the hell off my land. I want nothin ta do with you. And my wife don't want nothin ta do with you." Jakob was so angry that he kicked the ax he was using to split wood and it tumbled to the bottom of the wood bin. "Now see what you made me done. Git out of here," Jakob screamed as he put a nearby ladder into the wood bin and went down to retrieve the ax."

Eva jumped off her horse and ran to the wood bin just as Jakob threw the ax out so he didn't have to carry it up the ladder. She was seething with anger and saw her chance to get back at him. Without stopping to think about what she was about to do, Eva pulled the ladder up, slammed the lid shut, and locked it from the outside with two substantial latches.

"You can just sit down there and sweat until someone comes by and lets you out. I hope that doesn't happen for a long time."

Jakob was suddenly in the dark and afraid. He was only 5'4" and 130 pounds, so he could not put any leverage on the lid from the floor of the bin, and there were not any wood pieces long enough to reach the lid in an attempt to ram it open.

Jakob yelled to Eva to let him out. "My wife ain't here. She left and gone to Iowa yesterday fer two weeks to visit her sister." But Eva had mounted her horse and left. After a few minutes he started screaming at the top of his lungs, but there was no neighbor close enough to hear his screams. Eventually, he lost his voice and could only whisper.

A person can exist for three weeks without food but barely three days without water. Jakob lay down on the floor to conserve energy and hope against hope someone would come by or Elizabeth would come home early. He listened intently to any sounds outside the bin, but no one came by. His was a slow and frightful death. By the end, he had become as insane as Rebecca in Augusta. I savored both the irony and the justice of his death, but yet I had a trickle of compassion for Jakob; it was a terrible way to die.

In the meantime, Eva worked her way back to Minneapolis and stopped for a day to visit her father before heading back to Augusta – as she said she would. She told Charles about her locking Jakob in the wood bin and hoped his wife was visiting friends for the day so he'd suffer some. "Mother had wanted something bad to happen to Jakob, and now I've fulfilled her wish for revenge." Little did Eva know at the time how complete the revenge would be.

There was no remorse in her telling the grizzly story, no anxious looks, no expressing whether what she did was right or wrong. She did what needed to be done and that was it. And yet her father loved her and told her he'd protect her if Jakob came looking for the step-daughter who locked him in the wood bin.

When Elizabeth returned home from Iowa after two weeks, on June 4, it took her little time to find Jakob. The smell coming from the wood bin was overpowering. She opened the lid, saw Jakob, and quickly shut it again, walking to a neighbor's house to stay until the police came to remove the body and investigate the case. Determining the day of death was not an exact science in those days. A coroner declared that Jakob died on May 24, whereas he actually died on May 25, for I was with him at the bottom of the wood bin and knew he had lasted for three days, not two.

Since the ladder was out of the bin and Jakob could not have locked the lid from below, murder was the declaration, but no suspect was ever found. Eva had come into Rockford and left unseen, like a ghostly grim reaper. Charles found out about Jakob's death from one of his clerks who had relatives nearby, and realized that Eva had not just punished Jakob by locking him in the wood cellar; she had killed him – and he carried the secret to his grave.

During a now rare lucid moment for Rebecca, Eva told her mother about locking Jakob in the wood shed. Her mother laughed and clapped her hands, and Eva laughed with her and bestowed on her a warm hug. Those were Rebecca's last signs of the recognition of reality, and she retreated into her madness without relief until she died in 1880.

When Elizabeth married Anton Schaar, August 12, 1865, Charles sent a letter to Eva in Augusta to tell her Jakob had died in his wood bin and his house was now sitting empty and perhaps she could claim it if she talked to Elizabeth and told her she was Jakob's daughter. "Then you would be close to me and perhaps we could find an asylum for Rebecca in Minnesota." Eva had not meant to kill Jakob, but she felt no remorse that he had died a horrible death.

Eva sensed a change of scenery would be good for her, so that fall she returned to St. Paul, found out from her father where Anton Schaar lived in the Medina area, and took a stagecoach to visit Anton and Elizabeth.

"I know this will be a shock to you, Elizabeth, but I am Jakob's daughter from his first marriage. Here's my birth certificate." She shrewdly withheld from them that Charles Gravely was her real father.

"Your father told me of you Eva, but he didn't say much about you. He was not talkative about his past. You are a beautiful young lady; your mother must be proud of you."

"My mother is in an insane asylum in Maine and doesn't recognize me anymore, and now my father is dead. I don't know what to do." Eva, calculating that they would take pity on her, said nothing more.

Elizabeth and Anton excused themselves and went into the kitchen to talk.

"Anton, I feel sorry for that girl. Could we deed the house over to her and keep the land? Anton was a generous and wealthy man and agreed to Elizabeth's proposal.

Eva moved into the house the following spring, was generously helped out by Anton and Elizabeth until she met the local lawyer, 24-year-old Alexander Gant, and married him on her sixteenth birthday in 1867. This was the start of the Gant lineage that occupied the house for the next 139 years until Eldridge was murdered that fall day in 2006.

Gertrude Schaar visited her stepsister Eva in 1880, a few days before Gertrude was to be married to Christian Ackerman and a few weeks since Gertrude's mother Elizabeth had told her she was Jakob

Meyer's daughter and not Anton's. Charles Gravely was also visiting that day, and Gertrude recognized a strong resemblance between Eva and Charles, like father and daughter she later told a friend. Soon after that visit, Charles met an untimely death when he was struck down by a runaway horse and wagon in the dusty streets of St. Paul.

After her marriage, Gertrude's and Christian's house was less than five miles from Eva's and Alexander's, and they made polite visits back and forth every now and again. It bothered Gertrude that Eva spoke so despairingly about Jakob whenever the topic of their mutual father came up. One day, in a fit of frustration, Gertrude confronted Eva with an allegation that she was the daughter of Charles Gravely and not Jakob Meyer. Eva went into such a fit of rage that she cursed Gertrude and told her she had no proof of such an accusation. Gertrude smiled and said, "That's what I thought."

When Elizabeth died in 1895, Eva petitioned the War Department for Jakob's pension and received it in 1896. Armed with what her mother had told her and the confrontation above, Gertrude claimed *she* was the legitimate heir to receive the pension because Eva was Charles Gravely's daughter, but she had no proof. She tried again in 1905 and stated in a deposition that Eva was not Jakob's daughter, but without proof she did not prevail.

Eva died in 1931 of esophageal cancer at the age of 80, and Gertrude tried once more to claim the pension with a letter to President Roosevelt in 1934, to no avail.

As I promised to reveal, that's the mystery of who killed Jakob Meyer and why. Anna, Jack, and law enforcement agencies will never know the story. No one ever will but me, Time.

CHAPTER FIFTEEN

THREE MONTHS LATER

Anna and Jack were at their usual table at Murray's on a Saturday night, August, 18, 2007. A short-term severe storm was passing through Minneapolis, and the thunder was so powerful it rattled the dishes at the back of the restaurant.

Jack held Anna's hand and looked into her eyes with bottomless love. "Anna, my darling, have I ever told you how much I love you?"

"I'm not certain you ever have, my dear," responded Anna with a twinkle in her eyes. "Do you love me enough to marry me?" Anna was engaged in her Irish brand of playful sarcasm.

"Why, yes I do, Miss Fitzgerald."

Jack had stumbled unaware into Anna's calculated trap. "Doesn't it seem a trifle long to wait five more months of courtship before we can become engaged, and then how much time will pass until we're married?"

Jack clearly understood Anna was challenging the one-year courtship proposed by his father and agreed to by both of them, and he didn't want to travel that path, so he did what men have done for ages – he changed the subject. He sat back in his chair in a relaxed manner, folded his arms across his chest, and said, "Let's deal with what we agreed to cover over dinner tonight – the Decree of Descent your received yesterday naming you the sole heir to the Civil War coins, to Eldridge Gant's house, and its contents."

Well, Anna and Jack knew what events had led her to receiving the Decree; but to make it clear to everyone, I'll connect the dots of what happened over the past three months.

After Eldridge was murdered on October 16, 2006, a lawyer in Buffalo, Minnesota, contacted the Sheriff's Office of Hennepin County and made known that he held the will of Eldridge Gant and wondered how he should proceed in legally presenting it to all parties named in the will, given that the person who had bequeathed his estate to a relative had been murdered. Lieutenant Daily of the Investigative Division contacted Billy Wadie, the lawyer, and told him an investigation was in progress and he should hold the will until the case was closed, and so he did.

On May 18, 2007, Jack Quinn paid a visit to Billy Wadie, requesting to see the will, explaining he was representing Anna Fitzgerald. Billy pompously said, "I have been directed by the Sheriff's Office of Hennepin County to hold the will until the case is closed, and that's exactly what I'm going to do."

"What about the practice of offering a courtesy review for a colleague?"

"I don't know you; you're no colleague of mine, and I won't let you examine the will."

Billy Wadie sat behind his desk with a sneer on his face. Jack, in his anger, moved toward him as if he were going to punch the sneer off his face, then backed up and left Billy's office.

Next Monday, Anna and Michael O'Hara arrived at Mr. Wadie's office with a search warrant for Eldridge Gant's will. He hesitated, and Michael, who knew what had happened to Jack last Friday, had some harsh words for Billy.

"I'll tell you what, my friend, if you don't supply that will in five minutes, we will arrest you on probable cause for Obstructing Legal Process and haul you off to the Hennepin County brig. You'll be featured on the front page of the Buffalo newspaper, and if I were the judge, I would suspend your license until you learned to respect the law."

Billy wasn't accustomed to anyone confronting him like that. It hurt his pride. He glared a hateful glare and said nothing in return, walked to a back filing area, and produced Eldridge's will within five minutes.

The will was not lengthy, and it was as Jack had prophesized four days before: everything Eldridge had was bequeathed to his nephew Lucius, with a declaration that under no circumstances were Lucius' children, Jimmy and Jacob Gant, to obtain any of his property. That was it. Eldridge was old and not able to foresee any other possibilities, and Billy was too sloppy a lawyer to suggest that if Lucius died before Eldridge (or in this case was excluded from the will because he arranged for his uncle's murder), and if his estate was not to go to Jimmy and Jacob, who would it go to, given that Eldridge had no other living relatives?

Nevertheless, the probate court administrator had advertised in the Minneapolis StarTribune for other interested parties to Eldridge's inheritance, as required by law. As usual in such cases, several people called in to say they were a descendent in the Gant lineage. One person was an inmate in a maximum-security prison who had murdered his wife's father and mother to speed up the inheritance his wife would receive. Another was a woman of pure Chinese descent who claimed her last name was Gant. The oddest one was a woman 88-years old who claimed she was the daughter of Eldridge Gant, which would make Eldridge nine-years-old when he fathered her. And there were seven others.

Each one's story had to be checked out thoroughly, and in the end, all were proven to be false. It took considerable time.

Two months later the probate court determined that Lucius and his two sons were the only interested parties who could legally contest Anna's Decree of Descent – which Anna had petitioned the probate court for shortly after she and Michael had reviewed Eldridge's will. It was time to read the will, and the Sheriff's office proclaimed so to Billy Wadie.

Lucius, by Minnesota Statute, was not lawfully eligible to receive anything. Jimmy and Jacob Gant were called in for the reading of the will, and the probate court appointed Jack Quinn to be at the reading as Anna's lawyer, protecting her interests. When Jimmy and Jacob found out they were written out of the will, they were not surprised; they knew Eldridge disliked them, and the feeling was mutual.

Jack asked them if they would contest the will or contest the Decree of Descent naming Anna as the sole heir to the Civil War coins and the house and all its belongings. The brothers asked if they could talk privately.

Jimmy spoke first. "Jacob, I don't want any part of Eldridge's assets, even the Civil War coins worth nearly 2 ½ million dollars, because our father killed his uncle. I may have run drugs, but I never killed anyone. I admit initially I had wanted Eldridge roughed up to obtain those coins, but I gave no instructions to murder him. That was our father's idea."

"Jimmy, I doubt our contesting the will or Anna's right of descent would go anyplace anyhow. Anna gave me a heads up to let me know she had filed for a Decree of Descent, and she showed me the evidence she presented to the probate court to make her case, which, from my point of view, was iron clad. It included exhuming three bodies to prove that a person named Gertrude Ackerman was the only legitimate heir to Jakob Meyer's property and not Eva Gant, who stands at the head of our lineage. It was legally convincing and I don't think we'd stand a chance in contesting either the will or Anna's claim to being sole heir. I say we bow out gracefully and sign a document saying we will not contest." And that's what happened.

Let's return to Anna and Jack at the dinner table.

"So what do we do now, Jack, my darling?"

Jack became quite lawyer-like and seemed to have something else on his mind. "You need to make a final decision of what to do with the Civil War coins, Eldridge's house, and its belongings."

"Why, Jack," said Anna in amusement, "you have changed from lover to lawyer. I liked it much better when you were the lover."

Jack was obviously embarrassed. "I'm truly sorry, Anna. I'm a bit of a chameleon sometimes. I like it better when I'm a lover also."

Anna had a sweet smile on her face. "I was only kidding you, Jack. If you were always the lover, I think I would tire of you."

That was an interesting exchange. I have always felt different subjects demanded different personas, just as a CEO of a large corporation is a loving father as he kisses his little girl on the way out of the house; and by the time he arrives at the office, he has assumed the personage of a no-nonsense businessman and later becomes a decisive tiger when there is a critical budget item to decide. That's just the way it is. Jack's role had changed from lover to lawyer as it should have, but he took too seriously Anna's light-hearted chiding of him. I can only deduce that something was bothering him and his sense of humor had suddenly faded.

"Well, Jack, I have already decided what to do with the Civil War coins. I have researched disabled veteran's charitable groups, and one that is highly rated is Disabled American Veterans Charitable Services Trust. As my pro bono lawyer, would you be willing to liquidate the coins into cash and make a donation in my name to DAV?"

With a more laid-back lawyer voice, Jack said, "That is an excellent charity; I'm familiar with what they do and that less than 3% of the money they bring in goes to administrative expenses. You've made a good choice. And, yes, I will take care of those two matters for you."

"Thank you, Jack. That leaves Eldridge's house and belongings to decide about. I haven't given as much thought to that as to the coins, and anyway I think it's something you and I need to talk about as we plan our married future."

Jack appeared nervous, and Anna did not fail to notice. "What's wrong, Jack, are you feeling all right? You look like you have the jitters."

"It was a day of critical events for me, Anna; that's all, and the implications of those events make me uneasy. I'll be OK, but I think I could use some fresh air. Our waiter said the storm has passed, and we could wander around downtown Minneapolis for a while if you don't mind."

"I don't mind at all. I'd like some fresh air too, and right after a storm is a refreshing time."

When the bill was paid, Anna and Jack wove a winding path through the tables that separated the back of Murray's from the front. When they reached the front door and looked out, the storm had indeed passed, taking the high humidity away and creating a beautiful night for a walk.

They took a left on 6th Street, walked a block, and turned right on Nicollet Mall. Within three blocks, they stood before a jewelry shop that had a wonderful window display of diamond rings. Jack casually said, "Maybe we should start researching engagement rings; the time to be engaged is just around the corner, a few pages of the calendar."

"Five pages on the calendar to be exact, Jack," said Anna with a sigh, "and that doesn't seem just around the corner to me ... but it might be fun to see what's available and maybe the looking will give me hope."

"How about that one as an engagement ring?" mentioned Jack, as he pointed out a beautiful ring in the middle of the display. The diamond in the ring was large enough to be substantial without being ostentatious. It's what they had agreed upon early in their courtship days.

"That's a precious ring, Jack. I'd be delighted to wear it."

"Let's see what it looks like on your hand."

"I thought we were just looking."

Jack smiled weakly. "You seem to like the ring; let's see if you still do when it's on your ring finger."

"I guess that's a good idea, Jack," said Anna with a girlish tone to her voice.

They walked in the front door and were greeted by the owner of the store. "Anything I can help you with?" he asked.

"Could Anna try on that ring?" replied Jack, pointing to the one he and Anna had been looking at.

The owner pulled out the chosen ring and placed it on Anna's left hand ring finger. It was a perfect fit. "I love it," said Anna. "This is exactly the ring I want."

Jack was more jubilant than I would have expected. "Could we put that ring on hold for a number of months with a down payment? Or would it be easier for you to order the same ring in five months?"

"There is no 'same ring' as this one. It's one of a kind I'm afraid, and I have another piece of bad news for you. I would have been willing to put it on hold, but it's already been purchased by a gentleman just today. Sorry. Would you like to look at other rings?"

"No," replied Anna, with a cloud of disappointment in her voice. "I don't see anything I like nearly as well. We'll just have to continue looking; after all, we have five months." The last sentence was issued with low-key sarcasm, not intending to hurt Jack but more of an expression of her own frustration. Anna took the ring off and handed it to the owner.

Anna was ready to leave the jewelry store, but Jack had one last question to ask. "Who bought the ring today, if you don't mind my asking?"

The owner held the ring in his hand. "I'd have to look at my records for the full name, but the first names of the couple are engraved on the inside of the band, near the top of each side. Do you want to see who it is?" The owner directed his question to Anna.

"Sure," answered Anna with disappointment in her voice but a sense of curiosity. "Just today; what bad luck."

If you looked up the word "dazed" in the dictionary, there would be a picture of Anna with the look on her face she had just then. The names on the inside of the ring were "Anna" and "Jack."

"B…but I'm Anna," burst forth a stammering voice, "and this is Jack."

"I know," said the owner. "Congratulations."

Jack tenderly took the ring from Anna and dropped to one knee. "Will you marry me, my darling? I couldn't wait another five months either, so I decided to bend the rules of the courtship."

Anna was so dumbfounded she couldn't speak, but the tears in her eyes said much.

Jack was laughing by this time and stood up. "I believe it's customary that the one being proposed to says either yes or no."

"That *is* how it's done," said the owner with a smile.

Anna put her arms around Jack's neck, and in so doing her feet were no longer on the ground as she shouted out, "Yes, yes, yes. Oh yes. I love you, Jack. I will be a good wife to you."

"And I will be a good husband to you." Jack put his arms around Anna's waist and gently let her down to the floor, then put the ring on her finger.

As they departed the jewelry store, Anna turned to Jack with passion in her eyes. "Well, Mr. Quinn, when should we set the date to be married?"

"We'll talk about that tomorrow, Mrs. Quinn."

My name is Time. I have witnessed the history of the world unfold since Genesis, and I will be there to observe the last days as described in Revelation. With all the wars, famine, and catastrophic events cascading throughout the pages of history, Anna's story has been pleasing for me to watch, and I have accurately reported it.

This seems a good place to end for this part of the story. I don't know what will happen to Anna tomorrow or when her marriage to Jack will take place, but I will be watching it all closely.

CPSIA information can be obtained at www.ICGtesting.com
Printed in the USA
LVOW12s1438111013

356554LV00002B/442/P